JUSTIFIABLY
WOUNDED

MARK
ROEMMICH

Justifiably Wounded
Book 1 of the Justifiably series

Copyright © February 2015 R. S. Publishing
Published © February 2015 R. S. Publishing

ISBN-10: 099092890X (paperback)
ISBN-13: 978-0-9909289-0-4 (paperback)

Cover Art Designed By: Book Cover By Design
Editing & Formatting By: S. H. Books Editing
Services

DEDICATION

I have heard that people come into your life for three
reasons: a reason, a season, or a lifetime.

With that being said, I would like to thank everyone
who has made their way into my life, whether it was
by invitation or fate.

TABLE OF CONTENTS

TABLE OF CONTENTS

ACKNOWLEDGMENTS

"The greatest discovery of my generation is that human beings can alter their lives by altering their attitudes of mind." — William James

To Mark–Thank you for helping me take my weirder than fiction life and placing it into something beautiful, poised, and elegantly scribed. Our meeting was destiny. You are an amazing example of true talent, and I am so touched you are the one who was sent to me to make my dreams a reality.

To my inner circle who knows the real me and has loved me anyway. Thank you for the support you've shown me during this process.

To my family, for always being there. I was not an easy child, young adult or adult. Hell, I'm surprised you still talk to me! You showed me tough love when I needed it and was there when I finally decided to turn things around.

To my children–I want to thank you for always loving me, no matter the decisions I have made in my life. Even the decisions that have affected you directly. You are living proof that I must have done something right in my life, and without the love and support from all of you, this would have never been possible. You have shown me the meaning of unconditional love. May the one lesson I teach you from my life be to never give up on your dreams. Everything is possible with hard work, determination, and perseverance.

~ Raquel Syrah

Justifiably Wounded

"I find hope in the darkness of days, and focus in the brightness . . . I do not judge the universe."

DALAI LAMA

PROLOGUE

LOS ANGELES, THE CITY OF ANGELS, is a false dichotomy, a formal place consisting of many failures and successes, hiding its true identity in the shadows. The two entities are present as if they are exhaustive, when, in fact, other alternatives are possible. In some cases, they may be presented as if they are mutually exclusive, or they might be found in the dark belly of the city.

Although, there is a broad middle ground, Raquel Syrah resides in this space, searching for her true identity. Raquel, in the purest of forms, is a free spirit born to this city, and has survived the streets and the baggage bestowed upon her by her mother. She will inherit some of this baggage as her own and accept it, but some she will reject and store it away in a place labeled 'bad luck.'

A train wreck has more order than this girl's life, at times. The question that haunts her is, can a child pre-determine its course, or does judgmental society do it for her? She won't be able to answer this question for a very long time, if at all. She survives, and although her story might not be as abusive as many, she prevails. She chose to shape her own destiny and that is all that's important to her. She has and will continue to travel, but she will always return to her base or nest. They say that you can never go home, but that's also part of the dichotomy of life. Some just cannot survive in the outside world. Perhaps Raquel is one of those.

****

MOST OF LOST ANGELES is still asleep. The only sound prominent today and every morning is that of the street cleaners out in full force, removing the scum from the night's activities. Even the dark deviant slum areas of Los Angeles Street remain asleep, except for a few homeless still searching for a resting place or a quick fix. It would not be unusual to see the weak bent over at the waist, receiving an anal probe so that he might get his fix for the day.

In contrast, not too far away is the Mission about to open its doors. A small line is forming from the street population. They know to get there early for their food, or the wait will be long and cold. It's 6:30 AM in the City of Angels, and there is an onshore mist coming from Santa Monica beach, covering the city in a blanket of dampness.

Vacationers visit Los Angeles for the beaches and sunshine. Some come to visit Hollywood in hopes of seeing their favorite star. Most go away with sunburn and sand in their luggage. Then there are the thousands every year who come here to be discovered, to make their fame and fortune overnight. Most go away with sunburn, sand in their shoes, and the major disappointment that they might be just ordinary and not star material.

Some even fall victim to the temptations that come with fame and fortune seeking. Because of this, they will map out a path to the Twin Towers. Yes, Los Angeles has its own Twin Towers. It's part of the downtown skyline. For those of you who do not know about the famous Twin Towers of LA, it's the residence of the most wanted, the casual thief, the senseless con man, vagrant, or maybe just the unfortunate that can't get their lives together.

Thanksgiving Day is approaching, and within the thick walls of these famous towers, sitting alone in the release tank is Raquel Syrah, a tall attractive blonde, approximately twenty-eight years of age. One might wonder what she is doing here. At first sight, she certainly doesn't represent the underprivileged or someone who would fall victim to crime or punishment. Just the same, she is here and she is alone, waiting for the sound of the door to click so that she is free once again.

Raquel should have been released hours ago, but her defiance delayed her freedom. She is not one to challenge circumstances, but just hours before she was to be released, she mixed it up with another inmate and it cost her solitude in this cold empty room.

She looks around the tiny room, wondering who she should call or where she should go. Nothing or no one comes to mind. She truly is alone. Perhaps she'll walk out those doors and a friend will be waiting in the parking lot for her. Maybe word has gotten around that Raquel Syrah is to be released today and a band of friends are just on the other side. But then, reality sinks in, and she knows there will be no one.

Then that all too familiar sound is heard. The door clicks and she is free. She has nothing with her, so there is no need to collect her belongings. She has only the clothes on her back. She wipes away the tiny tear that rolls down her cheek and walks toward the door. To her surprise, Katy, a former inmate is returning to the Towers to collect her belongings. She'd been released from custody at the courts, so she didn't have time to collect them the day before. She steps through the door and comes face to face with Raquel.

"Hey, girl, what up?" she asks.

A smile spreads across Raquel's face. Her wish has come true after all. The answer to her prayers has arrived, although it seems it has been delivered in the form of a Hyundai.

"Damn, girl, I had no idea what the hell I was going to do," she says.

Katy tells her to sit tight outside. She'll be right out after collecting her crap. Raquel gladly hits the door and she heads out into the brisk morning air.

She turns and looks up at the Towers one more time. "Fuck you!" she says as she slowly walks away.

Of course, the exclamation falls on deaf ears. Raquel is dressed in a casual, but expensive, outfit. A glimpse of skin flashes a map of tattoos that adorns her shapely body. There is a long history behind these tattoos, but that will be revealed soon enough. For now, let's just simply say that Raquel has spent fifty-one days in the Twin Towers, and today at 6:30 AM, she was released back to Los Angeles. She is, once again, free of the constraints of the daily routine of lab rat mentality and drill sergeant bureaucracy.

"Yes, you heard me, motherfucker!" she barks as she moves further away, giving the Twin Towers her middle finger one more time.

Raquel is no longer alone. She has a friend and that friend has a place for her stay. It probably isn't the best of circumstances, since that place will be invested with tweakers and drugs. She knows she won't be able to fight temptation and will most likely fall back, but right now, she has no choice. She knows to give it a few days and she will land on her feet. She will file for unemployment and get a job. That is the plan.

The door bursts open, and Katy emerges from the halls of justice. The Twin Towers soon loom in the distance. As soon as they hit the parking lot, Raquel is welcomed by two more of Katy's friends sitting in the car. The party of four then drives away.

Raquel takes a quick glance in the side mirror on

the passenger side. She can see the Twin Towers growing smaller as they move away. It doesn't really matter where she is going. It's more important to get away, to separate herself from the fifty-one days of inconvenience.

She knows she has the entire day ahead of her to figure out the rest. As they move away, tears begin to form and run down her cheeks, but she refuses to fall victim to self-pity. She certainly doesn't want her friends to see her despair. She forces a smile on her face, letting the world know that she is back and stronger than ever.

"What the fuck!" she whispers to herself, surrendering to the unknown that lies ahead.

****

IT ISN'T LONG before Raquel is back in a place where she feels safe. She's back in the valley, and although it represents everything she wants to forget, it's a safe place to fall until she figures things out. Her friend has rescued her from despair and brought her to a friend's house to chill. Katy's friend, Paul, is an older guy, and he somehow manages this amazing place. Wine and drugs are out in the open, and anyone is welcome to join in.

After the long stay in County, Raquel is sitting alone to the side, watching her friends enjoying themselves, fighting the urge to join in. *Why not?* she thinks, but then, reality kicks in and she remembers that she wants her previous life behind her.

Katy can see the concern and stress on Raquel's face. She comes over to talk to her, hoping to ease her trepidation.

"What's wrong?" Katy asks as she sits down.

"Nothing really. Thanks for yanking me out of the city," Raquel says with a small smile.

"You aren't staying?"

Raquel looks at her friend and feels that she should explain further, but she isn't sure she'll truly understand. "I can't."

Katy smiles and knows exactly why. Because of this, she doesn't press for an explanation. That's the way of this kind of world. People come and go. Sometimes, there are reasons, and other times, it just is what it is.

"You need a ride?"

Raquel is so happy that she doesn't have to justify her leaving. She's content about the fact that Katy is her friend and lets it go.

"No, I can walk. It's not far and I could use the air," she says. Raquel stands and hugs her friend. "Tell Paul thanks for taking me in."

She smiles. Raquel makes her way to the front door and turns one last time. Katy has rejoined the party. There is a moment, just a fleeting moment, where Raquel almost changes her mind, but she soon reaches for the doorknob and walks away.

****

RAQUEL HAS MAPPED out her retreat. She knows exactly where she is headed. Not far, perhaps a few blocks away, is an apartment building where another friend of hers lives. She grew up next door, and although she isn't certain that she will be taken in, she has to break away from Paul's and all that it represents. It means trouble and trouble is not what Raquel needs right now.

As she slowly makes her way through the neighborhood, she begins to recount all the things this place represents. She knows she's made the right choice. It's time to move on. She decides that she will find a job and do whatever it takes to make her own way without conflict or more chaos. That will be difficult, however, since she is still surrounded by everything she is trying to forget.

Raquel's confidence builds as she walks along. A smile appears on her face and her pace begins to increase. She is about to cross the street, moving toward her destination, when a black limousine appears and stops in front of her, cutting her off from the opposite side the street.

Raquel stops and waits for the rear window to open. It doesn't, but the back door swings open, offering her a ride. She looks around, wondering if this is just another bad decision. Perhaps it's the exit she's been waiting for. Sadly, there is no one to consult. She looks at the apartment complex and then back to the mysterious limousine.

"What the fuck?"

She surrenders and gets into the limousine. It soon pulls away.

1

LATER THAT NIGHT, a black limousine sits waiting in the underground parking structure of the Federal Building on Wilshire Boulevard in Los Angeles. Could this be Raquel's last stop? Did she find what, who, or where she was going?

Its engines are running and a chauffeur is standing near the back door with several secret service agents standing in key positions, securing the area. The elevator door opens, and a man, identity unknown, steps out with a cane in hand, escorted by two more secret service agents. There is no Raquel in sight. They walk him to the limousine, and he gets inside, the door swinging shut behind him. Moments later, the limousine pulls away.

It still remains a mystery. Is Raquel in this limousine? Could this be the same vehicle that picked her up at the Twin Towers? Perhaps not, since Los Angeles is home to many celebrities and high-ranking officials or politicians. Seeing a limousine is as common as seeing a Ford Escort in this city.

JUSTIFIABLY WOUNDED

The black limousine is followed by two black Escalade SUVs. It emerges from the underground parking lot of the Federal Building, and makes its way onto Wilshire Boulevard turning Eastbound. Immediately, one of the black Escalades moves in front of the limousine, and the other comes up close behind to safely guard the occupants of the vehicle.

Once again, the clouds have rolled in from the coastline, and downtown Los Angeles is a bit misty and cloudy. It won't keep the residency from venturing out into the nightlife, however. The black limousine makes it way along Wilshire Boulevard, drawing some attention as it passes Midtown, moving toward the center of Los Angeles. A news helicopter passes overhead, hovering a bit before moving away to the east.

****

THE HELICOPTER SWIFTLY MOVES along in search of more interesting headlines. The pilot listens to his instructions, and he moves toward the Warehouse District of downtown Los Angeles near the 10 Freeway. Large spotlights break through the clouds and mist, intersecting as though it is a sword fight. There is a special VIP benefit below, and the news station is not the only bird represented in the sky. All of the city's news stations are present for this black tie gala benefit being held in the newly renovated district.

A long line of black and white limousines are present. Famous celebrities and the prominent wealthy of Los Angeles are walking the red carpet. A strange demure is cast over this red carpet. All patrons are wearing masquerade masks made of gold or silver, concealing their true identities.

Oddly, there are no paparazzi or cameras anywhere on the ground near the heavily secured event. Large bodyguards secure the door, and no one passes if they are not on the exclusive list. Once again, it's a strange dichotomy. From the sky, the long expensive red carpet is seen spreading out into the darkness and the steel presence of the warehouse district.

****

AS THE MYSTERY PATRONS enter the warehouse, they are received by several waiters and waitresses. All are dressed in formal black attire, offering champagne and hors d'oeuvres.

"Champagne, sir?" the sexy waitress offers a handsome gentleman with a gorgeous brunette on his arm. One would guess that this arm candy is not his wife.

"Yes, thank you," he replies with a wink, much to the disappointment of his mistress.

The night is festive and there is an anticipated excitement in the air. The guest's identities are hidden, adding to the exhilaration of an already promising night.

Small groups gather, chatting about nothing but decadence and how much money they are making, who has screwed them over in Washington, and how they will get even in the end. Although, there are trays passing by, there are also several bars and tables arranged throughout the gallery that offer continued pleasures to the invited guests. Extravagant ice formations are the centerpieces for each table, surrounded by the most elegant of food.

This is definitely a special event and no detail has been spared. The wealthy patrons mingle, moving around the gallery hoping to catch an early glimpse of the anticipated art to be presented. Each display is hidden by surrounding curtains. The artist has requested secrecy until the last minute. The talk filtering through the crowd is a curious one about the new artist being presented for the first time in the United States.

"Baby, who is the artist again?" a beautiful escort says to her gentleman.

The gentleman is preoccupied with his conversation, and he responds quickly so as not to be rude. "He's some Italian guy, honey," he says, dismissing her and slightly turning his back on her.

The patronized escort takes a sip from her champagne and looks around for perhaps a more attentive eye. She locks eyes with a young-looking man with emerald green eyes peering at her through his sliver mask. These special evenings usually reside in a more famous theatre, but unpublicized events like this one only allow the top one percent of wealth to move secretly with their mistresses and boy toys without too much notice. No one talks or writes about these nights. For all intents and purposes, they don't exist. Events such as these are what they call "dream nights."

****

IN THE BACK ROOM OF THE GALLERY, the live art is getting ready. There are several artists known for body painting working on their individual models, both male and female. Each theme is unique and may represent any time in history. It can cross over barriers or periods of time. They can be contemporary, or they can be period.

"Hold still, baby," a very gay artist says to his model. He carefully sprays gold and silver paint along her magnificent body.

"Andre, I didn't move!" she retorts. "It's not my first time, baby."

Andre frowns and fights back. "Don't be a cunt, angel," he responds in his best snarly gay voice.

****

OUTSIDE, near the rear of the warehouse, the black limousine and SUVs pull to a stop in front of the building. Two secret service agents quickly get out and approach the back entrance of the gallery. One agent lifts his wrist to his mouth and makes their arrival known.

The back door immediately opens and the second agent opens the back door of the limousine. The mystery man exits. He pushes his white ivory cane out in front of him and is escorted into the gallery. The door is shut behind him. No one will be allowed in or out.

****

BACK INSIDE THE MAIN GALLERY, the crowd is active with anticipation and it is growing. Music plays in the background as the lights are adjusted. It's almost like a Broadway play. The curtain will go up soon, and all the preparation and anticipation will meet.

Standing to one side, lost in his boring world, is a boy toy with his older woman patron. She, too, is engaged in conversation, so he glances around the gallery for future prospects. He is the typical pretty boy who doesn't really care who he escorts as long as she spends plenty of money and falls asleep with her prescribed medication before he has to perform. He will then exit quietly in search of a more suitable lay. Most likely, he will service up his manhood to Alicia, the kitchen help, once the mansion goes dark.

Champagne and hors d'oeurves are being served. Behind each curtain, the artist is putting his finishing touches on his art. The crowd moves closer in anticipation of the reveal. The music begins to build, letting the crowd know that the show is about to begin. At the right moment, every piece will be unveiled simultaneously. The master of ceremony, also masked, steps in to immediate applause from the guests. He smiles and waits for the applause to finish and the music to lower.

"Welcome, everyone, to this exciting night. Thank you. Please, you're attention, please! Thank you. This is a very special night for Ramon Arturo and Starlight Galleries." He pauses, for a moment, for a small amount of applause. "It is Ramon's first visit to this country. We hope you will enjoy and appreciate his unique talents as much as we do, and, of course, we hope you will spend a lot of money."

Laughter erupts around the room as he steps away from the spotlight. The lights lower to special lighting as the music comes back up.

"Ladies and gentlemen, Starlight Galleries presents Ramon Arturo's, Living Passion," the master of ceremony says into the microphone.

When the special lighting and music reach their respective levels, the hidden areas showcasing Ramon Arturo's works are unveiled around the room. The crowd reacts with mixed reviews. Some are extremely favorable with huge applause. Others are shocked beyond belief and turn away immediately.

All of the themes are uniquely different, but they are similar in the fact that the featured elements are all

LIVE NUDES, living art. All are of a sexual nature with nude men and women (artists/models) as the essence of the themes of passion. Some of the patrons leave immediately, but most remain and make their way to their favorite theme with voyeuristic interest.

The featured boy toy and his older woman patron are viewing the "bondage art theme" with extreme interest, more so her than him. The female model is hanging from the rafters by a long silk rope and her sexual body paint reveals lightning bolts and thunder clouds. She moves to the featured music and sound effects orchestrated for this theme. Her mask is painted on and her exquisite body moves as though the lightning is hitting her. She twists and turns, enacting the pain being inflicted on her, or perhaps, it is desired pleasure.

The male model is on his knees beneath her. He moves his hands up and down her body, stroking her thighs, reaching for her breasts. He then moves down, opening her legs so that his tongue can find her wet swollen pussy. He slowly kisses her thighs from side to side until he finds the moisture that draws his hard tongue. His hot wet tongue is inserted inside her, licking and drinking the nectar as it showers him. She screams as the sound of lightning and thunder hit a crescendo that matches his tongue's strokes. He dances his tongue on her clit and she screams out.

The boy toy stands staring at the performance

while his patron slowly slides her hand inside his pants to massage his thickening cock. He does not move as she would anticipate, but his breathing begins to build. As she moves her hand along his cock, he turns his head to the side, and his attention is immediately drawn to someone standing a few feet away.

He catches a glimpse of a gorgeous body elegantly dressed in a silver gown adorned with a silk hood and his breathing increases. His patron accepts his arousal as if she is the catalyst. He stares until the gorgeous body slowly turns toward him. Her crystal blue eyes peer out from behind the silver mask that hides her identity.

Once again, we are introduced to Raquel Syrah. She is a pure contradiction to the Raquel we saw this morning outside the Twin Towers. She turns away from the boy toy and focuses her attention on the sexual act being presented.

The male model's hands and tongue move with the music and the movement of the female model's body as she fights the thunder and lightning striking, driving her toward a climax. The male model doesn't hide his own enthusiasm for the performance. His manhood rises with each stroke of his tongue. Because the female model is in bondage, he slides his right hand down and begins to pleasure himself, forcing himself to match her ecstasy.

As he massages her clit with his tongue, her movement and moaning begins to overpower the sound effects of the thunder and lightning. She drops her head back and arches her back as he explores the inner wall of her wet pussy. She lifts her leg over his right shoulder and presses against his back, bringing him closer to her wet nest. The crowd reacts with "ahhssss" and moans.

Raquel watches with personal interest. Her own emotion begins to match the theme. She turns to face the boy toy who is still staring in her direction. She isn't interested and moves away as though she is in "slow motion." Her body and dress move majestically through the crowd until she finds herself standing in front of another theme.

Raquel stops and turns around to steal another glance. She can see the boy toy through the crowd, his eyes still locked on her body. She seductively and sadistically smiles, driving him to whisper something to his patron. She immediately draws her hand from his pants. He then moves through the crowd, heading in Raquel's direction.

This is a game she plays. It's as though she deliberately draws him into her web. Raquel's narcissistic beauty pulls him away from the wealth and power he enjoys toward an undiscovered conquest. This makes her happy. It is an obvious move, of course. Raquel has no choice when she becomes aware of any unambiguous glare or motive. Being very capricious, she stares straight ahead as he nears. He turns and stares at the display with added interest.

This particular theme features a nude Cleopatra sucking the large rod between the nude Marc Anthony's legs, while a handmaiden kisses and licks Cleopatra's inner thighs, reaching up to her lips.

"When history was at its best, wouldn't you say?" the boy toy whispers, hoping for a name and number.

Raquel begins to laugh out loud, blowing him off immediately with insolence so punishing that he cringes in embarrassment. She has reduced him to ashes.

"That's it? That's the best you can do?" she retorts. Her cruel sarcasm drives him back a few feet as heads turn in their direction. "My God, where do you poor fools learn this shit? I think you better stick with what you have. She is willing to pay."

The boy toy quickly moves away, feeling shattered. As he pushes through the crowd, he notices that everyone around him has overheard the crushing commentary, and they are now whispering and laughing. It has even drawn the attention of his older woman patron. He looks back at Raquel as he moves away.

"Bitch, as if you could afford me!" he bitterly says, trying to restore his pride.

Raquel laughs as she sees him rejoining his patron. They quickly move away to another area of the gallery. The entire time, he tries to calm his patron, but she remains upset by his overtures toward Raquel, the much younger, more beautiful woman. More importantly, however, is the fact that he has embarrassed her among her constituents.

At that moment, a short rock star type of guy named Billy breezes past them. He moves through the crowd toward Raquel. Billy approaches her, clutching two glasses of champagne. He hands one to Raquel, and receives a very affectionate smile in return. Everyone around them is still glaring at her. Billy soon notices this. The whispering has not subsided.

"What the fuck, babe?" he asks. "What happened?"

"Nothing, really," she replies. "They don't appreciate art when they see it, I guess." Her comments draw some disgust and several people move away.

He accepts her answer and turns his attention to the presentation. "Wow, love it!"

"Been there, done that. Let's move on."

He happily follows her as she makes her way from theme to theme. They joyfully move through the crowd, exchanging darting innuendoes as they slowly move throughout the gallery. Their conversation is flirtatious, light, and never heard.

Their body movements speak volumes. It tells us that they are in their own world, as if they are the main theme of the gallery. They pass by the older patron and her boy toy, once again, and they can feel their wintry stares. A secret service agent approaches Raquel and the rock star, and whispers something in Billy's ear. Billy, in turn, whispers to Raquel. She is lured away and follows the agent out of the main gallery, leaving the rock star on his own.

****

RAQUEL AND THE AGENT silently make their way down a long hallway. They approach the door of a private room near the back of the gallery. The agent stops and whispers to Raquel, and she shoots him a confused glance. She finds his instructions mysterious and questions him further for an explanation. Their exchange cannot be heard, but there is a sense that Raquel is uncomfortable with his answer. However, she submits to his instructions and reluctantly enters the room alone.

Raquel enters the dimly lit room, and the door is secured behind her. Once again, she feels jailed.

She looks around the dark, shadowed, and empty room, waiting for her eyes to adjust before moving forward. She can make out several art pieces against the far wall and some crates stacked near one end of the room. At the opposite end of the room is a beautiful Louis the XIVth loveseat. Seated on one end of it is the man from the black limousine. His identity remains a mystery to her as he sits in the dark shadows of the room.

He graciously invites Raquel to sit with him. "Raquel, don't be intimidated. Please, come and sit with me," he says in a mysterious soft voice.

"Men don't intimidate me, honey. I just don't

know you and I'm not accustomed to taking orders that well," she answers.

Raquel slowly walks to the middle of the room, finding this whole cloak and dagger scenario amusing, but ridiculous, at the same time. She stops and looks around the room as if she expects something out of the ordinary to happen.

"Raquel, humor an old man and come sit down. There is no one but you and me here. You have my word."

Raquel moves forward, showing no sign of fear, though she remains cautious. She approaches the mystery man, remaining in complete control just as she displayed earlier with the boy toy. With each step, she gains more and more control of her emotions. By the time she reaches him, she could slay a dragon.

"I relish cloak and dagger as much as the next guy, but this is a bit too Hollywood, Washington-like for me. Men always love this sort of thing . . . the little boy in them, I guess," she taunts.

The mystery man is amused and he laughs. "Perhaps, you're right, my dear. But I assure you, I have a purpose here."

He pats the loveseat next to him, inviting her to sit down, but Raquel is reluctant and feels that she can handle this situation at arm's length. She hesitates for a moment, and then decides to take a seat. Now, they both are hidden in shadows. She decides to remove her mask as their verbal combat begins.

"You're a very beautiful woman," he says as he

reaches over and touches her leg.

Raquel remains calm, but sends a direct stare in his direction. He quickly withdraws his hand, laughing a bit to diffuse the situation. She doesn't share the levity of his humor.

"And smart, I might add. You're like your Mama. Feisty, I like that," he adds, and suddenly, he has her attention.

"I hope you didn't call me in here to talk about my fucking mother," she says. "She's my least favorite subject."

She starts to get up. He grabs her arm, but quickly draws it away, remembering her earlier reaction.

"Please . . . Indulge me a little longer, Raquel. Just listen for a moment," he pleads.

Raquel remains standing, but she doesn't move away. "You get three minutes, and I mean three minutes. So I suggest you use them wisely."

The mystery man heeds her warning and quickly changes the subject. "You went to jail for him, and I want him. You give him to me, and I will change your life forever," he offers.

Raquel begins to laugh and her whole body reacts to the laughter. She can't believe that this whole masquerade is about an estranged boyfriend. She realizes that her good friend, Billy, the rock star, has been drawn into service to deliver her to this charade.

Okay, she thinks. *I've enjoyed the show, but betrayal is not my style.*

"This is more ridiculous than that poor pathetic bastard in the gallery. First of all, I didn't do time for a guy, and I don't have any idea what guy you're talking about. Secondly, if you did your homework, you'd know I don't roll over on my friends. Do you know what that would make me?"

The mystery man doesn't hesitate to answer. "Yes, and you're going to do it," he says.

"And why the fuck would I do that?"

Again, he answers quickly and decisively. "Because if you don't, you will never see your kids again."

"Never!"

Raquel isn't sure where this conversation is going, but she is becoming quite uncomfortable with the tone of his voice and his threats. Fear begins to rear its head. She wonders if this man is powerful enough to deliver on his threats, and decides to press for more information before burning this bridge.

"Listen, I've known some guys in my time, so who specifically are you talking about? And, for the record, I don't like men who hide in shadows."

"Miguel is the guy. His cut can be yours," he taunts.

Raquel is surprised to hear Miguel's name. She isn't used to wealthy powerful men offering Cinderella-type moments. She usually gets the bad boy who gives her 'the world is your oyster' type of dialogue that quickly dissolves after the climax. She doesn't understand why he would approach her about

Miguel.

"I don't see the connection."

"Help me with this small task and you get more than your fair share. More importantly, you'll get your kids back," he states.

Raquel laughs, amused by his attempt to up the ante. "Your three minutes are up."

"You be smart, Raquel. Make your own destiny. He's a fucking loser. He'd fuck you over in two seconds flat. I can be an ally, or I can be an adversary."

Raquel feels the sting of his words, but holds her composure. She is being given a chance to get out from under and turn her life around completely. *But what if I'm being manipulated into another dark cell?* she thinks.

"I know what you're thinking. 'What if I'm trading my freedom for thirty pieces of silver?' Well, I guess you'll have to take that chance," he says, and waits for her answer.

Raquel refuses to change her mind. She walks slowly toward the door, still thinking about the repercussions of her decision. Men have screwed her over before. *Is it worth losing my children?* she wonders. As she nears the door, she hears him bark one more taunt, and it echoes off the walls.

"You have a future with me, Raquel. All you have to do is . . . reach out and take it."

Raquel has definitely heard enough. She reaches for the door handle and hesitates for a moment, before she jerks it open and exits the room, closing the door behind her.

****

RAQUEL WALKS BACK into the crowded gallery and looks around for Billy. He is nowhere to be seen. He's done his job and has delivered her to the man. He is out of there, despite the entertainment.

As Raquel makes her way around the gallery looking for Billy, she can sense that all eyes are on her as though this whole night was a set-up. *Perhaps I am the main attraction,* she thinks.

Raquel wonders if everyone knows why she is there. She moves through the crowd, and they slowly form a path for her to the door. As she nears the door, she comes face to face with the boy toy, who is taking great satisfaction in her exit.

She shows no sign of concern or interest and walks past him, giving him a slight shove on her way out. She knows that she has to find Billy, to find out what the fuck the night was all about. Raquel shoves past the security, leaving the gallery, feeling unflappable, yet burning up inside with anger.

****

RAQUEL WASTES NO TIME in finding Billy. It was quite easy, actually. He's just like every other celebrity in Hollwood. He hangs out at Chateau

Marmont. His most recent success on the charts allows him VIP status, and he occupies one of the penthouse suites. This famous hotel reached star-studded status when they barred Lindsay Lohan from the premises.

She arrives in a taxi and enters the hotel with a mission. Raquel bolts through the lobby and draws a lot of attention from almost everyone, especially since she is dressed to kill. As she nears the check-in desk, a good-looking actor type wannabe sidles up to her to lay down his best line. She sees him coming. Before the words are even out of his mouth, Raquel puts out his fire.

"Fuck off, limp dick. You can't handle this much woman," she states as she breezes past him on her way to the elevators.

Ignoring everyone around her, Raquel bangs on the button and the doors open. She steps inside and closes the door. The elevator starts up, taking her to where she wants to go.

****

RAQUEL EXITS the elevator and looks down the long hallway toward the penthouse suite. She has no idea if Billy is even there, but it's too late. Her wrath has driven her, thus far. There's no turning back now.

She makes her way down the long hallway and reaches the double doors, hesitating for a second. If at all possible, she would knock the damned door down, but she has been in enough trouble lately, so she knocks firmly on it instead. Raquel waits for a split second and bangs on it again, but with much more vigor.

"Open the fucking door, you faggot!"

Just as she is about to hit the door with her fists, it opens. Standing in front of her is a gorgeous model type with nothing on but a pair of panties. Raquel sweeps her eyes up and down her body, and realizes there is a bulge in the panties.

Okay, we found ourselves a heshe, she thinks. *Why not, if that's his freaky thing?*

She pushes past the nude lovely at the door, screaming out for Billy. "Billy, get your white ass out here!"

Raquel is immediately met by the private butler. She flies past him and begins to search for Billy.

"Miss, you can't go in there," he says.

Raquel abruptly forces her way around the suite and out onto the patio. There is a small party already in progress. She darts into the half-naked crowd, unannounced, and glances around, looking for Billy. Naked groupies with very large manufactured breasts are everywhere. She wonders where these kids find the money to get cosmetic surgery every other month. When someone is famous, the list of pounces is long and they are magnets. You don't have to find them, they find you.

She moves around the patio in search of Billy, much to the disappointment of the butler who is in hot pursuit. She looks to the right toward the spa and thinks she recognizes his bare ass, humping a totally wasted blonde who is about to drown. As the male ass thrusts forward, the blonde's head submerges. She darts for the spa and grabs the guy's shoulder, spinning him around. To her disappointment, it's not Billy.

"Sorry, dude. Hit it again, but don't drown the bitch," she jokes.

She breaks away and continues her search. Unable to find Billy in the alcohol and drug infested crowd, she moves back toward the suite.

****

RAQUEL RACES THROUGH THE SUITE, shoving off the persistent butler in pursuit. The guests are surprised, but not in shock, since they have seen and experienced it all before. Whispers begin to quickly circulate around the suite and they all start chanting for Billy. She charges up the spiral staircase to the master bedroom, and barges through the door to find Billy lying on the large bed in Hugh Hefner style. Guys and girls of all colors and sizes lie around him. He is face down in the crotch of the heshe Raquel met at the door.

"You fucking bastard! Get that shit tool out of your mouth and get over here!"

Billy slowly releases the cock in hand and glances under his arm pit at Raquel. "Baby, what the fuck?"

he objects.

"Everybody out!" Raquel screams.

"No, everybody stay where you are!" he counters.

He gets up and doesn't bother to cover himself. Billy staggers toward Raquel and falls at her feet just before he gets there. He begins to laugh and she can't help but to join him. He's a mess and she wonders if this is even worth it. She reaches down and helps him to his feet.

"What the fuck, love?"

She suppresses her laughter. "You fucking asshole! You delivered me to the establishment! What the fuck?"

He stares at her like he is trying to figure out what she just said. "The man?" he questions. "Oh, that fucking asshole? Yeah, well, he kind of had my balls in his hand. I owe a lot of fucking money to the IRS, babe."

Raquel wants to release all of her frustration on his face, then and there, but instead, she paces in a circle until she calms down. She then turns around to face him once more.

"You betrayed a friend, you fucking dick. I wouldn't have done that to you."

He stares at her, completely stoned, and has no idea what she is saying. She realizes it and shakes her head. She looks around the room at the staring faces.

"What's there to drink?" she asks.

Everyone starts to laugh. The heshe holds up a

bottle of Crystal.

****

THE NEXT MORNING, Raquel awakens and finds that she is still in Billy's bed with about five other people. Complete strangers, of course. She slowly lifts the covers and discovers that she is nude. She shakes her head and wonders when that might have occurred.

Her head is pounding from the excessive alcohol and whatever party treats she might have shared. Trying to search through last night's memory is a chore. All she can surrender or confess to is that she has, once again, fallen victim to the lust and excitement of the night.

She looks around the bed and wonders how many she might have played. *Doesn't matter,* she decides. She's enjoyed her first night out of jail and that's good enough for her. She will leave the mea culpa until later in life. She's alive and that's all that matters.

Raquel searches for Billy within the collage of bodies, and discovers his all too familiar ass peering out from under the pile. She lies back on the pillow to get more sleep. She will drill him later.

2

WHATEVER DREAMS Raquel had as a child have
been abruptly shattered by the last couple years of her
life. At twenty-eight years of age, she remains a
lifetime distance to the goal or finish line she dreamt
about as a young girl. In the process, she has lost
custody of her three children. She wonders where it
might have all gone wrong. There are huge gaps in
her memory of her early life in Southern California.
The age of eight doesn't exist in her memory bank.
Was she eight, is a constant torment for her.

A yellow cab pulls up to a rundown apartment
complex in a disintegrating neighborhood, population
. . . deprived. After her night of pleasure in Billy's
suite, reality sets in and Raquel is left with only one
option. She has decided to take refuge with the
mother of a childhood friend, if she will have her.
Her name is Mary and she lives in a one bedroom
apartment in a horrible neighborhood in Van Nuys.
The cabby impatiently waits for his payment, while
Raquel stares at the apartment complex wondering if

this is such a good idea.

"What are you going to do, lady?" he asks.

Raquel sits in the back seat dressed in her street clothes, the ones she wore when she was released from the Twin Towers twenty-four hours ago. She tucks her expensive silver gown into a large paper Vons bag and gets out of the cab to face the day. She hands the cabby his token, given to her by Billy.

"Keep the change," she says.

He gladly takes the twenty and drives away, leaving her there standing at the curb. *How ironic,* she thinks. *I've come full circle. Perhaps the Twins Towers weren't so bad, after all.*

She dismisses the thought. Who would choose to be in jail just because it has a clean rack and three square meals a day, *if* you were lucky enough to get a cell? The overcrowding forces some to sleep in the commissary and in whatever space is available. All of the large rooms are converted to barracks at night.

Raquel sucks it up and moves up toward the apartment. As she approaches, she hesitates once more. She senses darkness, a depression, about this place. She wonders if it's fear or just plain anger for the choices she's made. Raquel can hear voices on the other side of the door. It opens and she comes face to face with a young guy.

"Hey, some tattooed chick is out here," he says.

Raquel knows, then, that she is walking back into that void she often finds herself in. She has no choice but to do what she must do. She has her children to think about. She needs to find her kids, and if this is the price she has to pay, she will grin and bear it.

Mary soon comes to the door. "Baby girl, what the hell you doing here?"

Raquel smiles and her wish is granted. Mary rewards her with a huge hug and invites her in.

"Come on, baby, get in here."

Raquel steps inside and the door slowly closes behind her.

****

FOR THE NEXT FEW WEEKS, Raquel hits the streets in search of a job in escrow. This honest profession has always been her ace card to play when times are difficult. It has always been her mantra to work long days, long weeks, and then party just as hard on the weekends. Don't bite the hand that feeds you is a philosophy she's never forgotten.

Raquel soon secures a job as an escrow assistant in a small firm. It allows her to lay low until something else comes along. Unfortunately, she doesn't have a license or a car, therefore the public transport is her carriage. She knows she must be bonded to secure a full-time job for any length of time, so the constant changing of jobs is likely to be in the cards. She knows her felony record will haunt her for a while, but that's her reality and she will just have to deal with it.

Right now, she is grateful for the small couch in

the living room she's been given, even though the nights are not quite what she expected. The walls are thin and the cockroaches are huge. Any movement will send them scurrying across the floor, and the thought of them sharing the warmth of her bed is enough to force her to keep one eye open. The whole place is filthy and roach infested, and she knows that she can't stay long. She will suck it up for the time being, however, until something better comes along. Until then, she lies awake at night, listening to the chaos that surrounds her and the constant sounds of sirens.

To Raquel's surprise, Mary's son, David, appears out of nowhere. He is happy to see Raquel. She and David had a thing a long time ago. Although time seems to separate them at different points in their lives, they always seem to hook up.

Raquel is sort of happy to see him, too, except she knows David is a speed freak. That won't be good for her. Temptation is always her best friend. In the heat of the moment, she and David hook up, and she moves to the second bedroom. It's a move she regrets, but it gets her off the roach couch. After a few days of lust and tweaking, Raquel knows that this can't happen. David is David, and that's bad news for her.

After days of wrestling with her planned escape, Raquel arrives home from a long day and decides to tell Mary that she has to move on. Mary won't be a huge fan of this since Raquel is making a financial contribution to the roach infested house. If Raquel leaves, she becomes the sole provider and she can't have that.

"No, you have to stay, honey. David is out!" Mary says. "He's a speed freak, and I can't have that here. He's out!"

"I can't let you do that to him," Raquel responds.

Mary insists that it's final. She will deliver the news to him as soon as possible. They make their way to the second bedroom and shove open the door only to find David with his ass in the air between a pair of legs.

"What the fuck?" Raquel cries.

"Hey, baby. What you doin' home?"

A stone cold light invades Raquel's eyes. She's had enough.

"David, you take this fucking slut and get out!" Mary barks.

Raquel looks up and silently thanks the Good Lord for the golden intervention.

"David, get your ass up!"

Raquel doesn't bother to say another word and walks away.

****

THINGS CALM DOWN some after David hits the road. Raquel is grateful that Mary has given her sanctuary, but she knows deep inside that she should move on. After several months of riding the bus and bumming rides from friends, Raquel hooks up with another old boyfriend named Mikey.

She knows Mikey isn't right for her either. That there is no future with him, but she needs to move on from the place she now finds herself in. It sounds callous and selfish, but she is trying to survive. A conscience has no place in her plans.

Raquel hasn't forgotten about Billy's betrayal. Asking him for help is not possible at this time. She has pride and integrity. In her mind, he is no longer trustworthy. She also remembers the threat she received from the mystery man. She will have to think about that some more. Thirty pieces of silver is beginning to sound pretty good right now.

****

RAQUEL'S TIME at Mary's is a lifesaver. Her relationship with David had always been a hit and run, so there is no love lost there. Her focus now is on work and getting her own place.

Everything seems to be coming along nicely, except that she still hasn't been able to see her kids. Raquel is on probation and there are rules. There will be random drug testing and no contact with her children until her probation officer gives the okay.

****

AFTER TWO MONTHS OR SO, Raquel is able

to get a guest house of her own. It's a studio home and she pays about $900 a month, but that's okay, because she is making good money. As usual, she is bouncing from job to job. In this line of work, you must be bonded with the State, and that's not going to be possible because of her record. Once fingerprints are taken, her full identity would be discovered and she'd be out, so it's easier to just job hop.

The real estate business is booming. Raquel knows finding a new job will be easy. No sense in crying over a job lost when there is a new one staring at her in the face. Between the drug testing twice a month and the endless bus rides beating down on her, Raquel knows that it might be time to bury the hatchet with Billy and perhaps get some real help. With no other option, she calls him.

****

RAQUEL ARRANGES their meeting time at Chateau Marmont. She is ready to clear the air with her longtime friend. She will forgive him, but she will never forget the betrayal. More importantly, she needs to know about what the connection to the mystery man is and how it involves her estranged boyfriend, a man she hasn't seen since she went to jail.

She arrives at Chateau Marmont to find Billy standing on the curb next to a black limousine. Raquel wonders if this might be stage two of the betrayal. She can feel the darkness rising again that often paints her blood black.

The cab pulls up behind the limousine. Raquel steps out with a smile. Billy looks up, happy to see his friend again.

"Baby doll, what the fuck is up?" he asks.

He hurries over to see her. Billy wraps his arms around her and hugs her tight, grabbing her ass in the process. It's all she can do to remain upright.

"Take it easy, you dog!" she jokes.

Billy instructs one of his minions to pay the cab driver, and he ushers Raquel toward the limousine. "Come on, babe. We're late," he says, sounding excited and half-baked.

"Where are we going?" she asks with a small amount of concern.

"Just get in. It'll be fun."

Raquel isn't one to turn down a spontaneous invite. That has always been her problem. You know what they say about curiosity? Well, spontaneity falls in that category, too. She gets in, and the black limousine pulls away.

Next stop, Puerto Penasco, Mexico! *What the fuck?*

****

THE BEACH COMPOUND in Puerto Penasco, Mexico, once the hideaway for Al Capone, is off the beaten path for celebrities. Both Raquel and Billy love it because they can party hard and not put up with the normal tourists, and more importantly, no paparazzi. Under normal circumstances, this would be an exciting three day weekend for anyone, but the problem here is that Raquel shouldn't be leaving the county. She's definitely violating her parole by leaving the entire friggin' country.

It's very quiet in the hideaway, except for the sounds of the surf pounding the shoreline and a few seagulls searching for something to eat. Hideaways such as this one don't come cheap. The privacy is a godsend, however. The French doors to the beach are open, and a warm tropical breeze enters the master bedroom.

There is no sign of Raquel or Billy. Her clothes are strewn across the bed, and there are several empty bottles of Crystal champagne scattered about the floor. Other than that, there is only the sound of the surf and wind accenting the room.

The private beach is empty. Raquel is spotted down near the water's edge and she is alone. She runs through the breaking water with laughter and play. It's as though all her worldly problems have been lifted from her shoulders.

Enjoying her freedom, she makes her way back up to the compound. For one second, she thinks that she will never go back, but then she remembers her kids and that makes this impossible. She has three small children and they mean more to her than any hideaway in Mexico.

She climbs the short wooden stairs that lead to the back of the house. Everything about this setting makes Raquel feel gorgeous. She is wearing only a red lace thong and her magnificent breasts are in full view. This is the first time her entire body is revealed. A long history of tattoos marks her body all the way down to her toes.

Raquel comes to a stop just outside the open French doors, enjoying several minutes of tranquility. She holds her beautiful hair in both hands as the wind blows around her body. She faces the dark ocean, feeling the heat and wetness between her legs, offering her breasts to whoever wants them.

Unbeknownst to her, Billy is standing just inside the door. He enjoys the erotic moment with her. Raquel, feeling a tad spooked, turns quickly to face the voyeur and discovers Billy instead.

"You scared the shit out of me. Where have you been?"

"Organizing a fucking party for us, baby," he says, holding up some booze and party treats.

"Fuck, we are the party, dude! So man up and give me that throbbing boner you're packing right fucking now!" she commands.

He laughs and drops his pants. Without a moment lost, Raquel is on her knees in front of him. She takes his member into her mouth, and begins to slide her tongue around the crown of his cock. He tilts his head back and howls. She then grabs his balls with one hand, and takes his cock down her throat.

"You nasty bitch!" he screams.

Raquel looks up at him and enjoys the torture she is inflicting on him. "There is some serious bondage coming, baby. I want every drop!" she promises, a reminder of the gallery night, her first night out of jail.

Billy loves her tongue and can't wait for the rest. Time seems to stand still, but it's only been minutes. Raquel is soon lying on her back, arms bound by drape cords, legs spread, shaking with adrenaline. Billy hovers over her, wanting desperately to penetrate her. Instead, he takes the empty Crystal bottle lying nearby and slides it between her wet lips. He can feel her muscles suck it in deep. She moans with excitement, pulling on the cords. He moves his thumb across her clit, teasing her as he moves the throat of the bottle in and out of her. Raquel's back arches and her breathing increases to match his strokes.

"Harder . . . baby . . . harder!" she commands with passion.

He removes the bottle, dripping in nectar, and offers her a drink. She tastes her sweet nectar, and she becomes even more aroused from the sweet scent of her own pussy. Billy takes the bottle from her lips, rubs it across her nipples and sucks them. He then lightly bites her hard wet nipples. She lets out a low growl from the back of her throat, like a wild feral beast.

Raquel tears her wrist from the cord. She rolls Billy off of her, and climbs on top of him. She slaps him across the face, and he enjoys the punishment.

"Come on, take it!" he screams.

Taking his erect shaft in her hand, Raquel toys with his hardness, which makes her desire all the more intense. Finally, with a firm hold, she thrusts him inside her. She arches her back to feel his cock's length and rocks him hard.

Roaring, Billy clenches his teeth as his eyes roll back into their sockets the harder she fucks him. The more intense the heat becomes between her legs. There is a magnificent display of pure brute force and she cums hard.

Raquel looks down at his ripped abdomen. She can see her juices squirting out, showering his hardness. With each squirt, he digs his nails into her firm ass. It doesn't get any better than this. Billy was looking for a party, and he got it all rolled into one woman.

His betrayal seems distant to Raquel now, but she hasn't forgotten it. She's known for her prowess and also for her insatiable sex drive. She is like a man when it comes to sexual exploits, and has no trouble stating that she fucks without emotion.

****

ON THE FLIGHT HOME, three days later, complete silence envelopes Billy and Raquel. It could be that they are totally exhausted, but it could also mean that there is an explosion about to happen.

Raquel is sitting alone, staring out the window, wondering if she still has a job. She still doesn't have answers from Billy about the mystery man and what his connection is to her boyfriend.

The time has come for her to clear the air. She looks over at Billy who's wearing his headset, listening to music. She reaches over and pulls the headset clear. He looks up and knows that the moment has arrived. Before she can ask, he delivers his confession.

"Listen, love, I owe the fucking IRS over a mil. The asshole put the squeeze on me," he confesses. "He wants your man friend bad, and he knows we are friends."

"So you throw me under the friggin' bus," she says in a low pained voice.

Billy shakes his head in denial. "I don't see it like that. I knew you could take care of yourself, so I did what he asked and my problem went away."

Raquel, quite disappointed with Billy, thinks for a moment before she says, "What does he want with Miguel? Fuck, the guy is a fuck up and can hardly hold a job. Besides, I haven't seen the guy for a long time."

Billy knows she is right, but he also knows there is a lot she doesn't know. He spends the next hour explaining to Raquel that the mystery man is more than just a three-piece suit. He has a ring of "providers," as he likes to call them. For safety purposes and insurance, the ring is made up of mostly small-time con artists or thieves, and fuck ups, but it is effective. This way he maintains his power over them.

He explains further that Miguel was brought in at the last minute on a job when one crew was light. At first, he seemed to be okay, but as time went by, his true self shone through. He is a greedy speed freak idiot and made too many mistakes. One night, he was busted because he didn't follow instructions. This did not go over well. He goes to court, and even with a serious rap sheet, he is given a short stay in County, all arranged by the mystery man.

"Are you telling me that Miguel could have done hard time and he got off because of this Fed dude?"

"Yep. Why do you think you fell through the cracks at County?" he says.

The light bulb turns on for Raquel. She's wondered how she was convicted on a bogus first degree burglary charge and only did fifty-one days. Especially, since she was on probation for an earlier offense of grand theft auto.

"Fate, fucking fate! Why not?" she yells.

"How did you meet the dumb shit, anyway?"

"My girl introduced us at a party. It just so happens, he is my ex's cousin. The dude puts his crosshairs on me, and we strike up a lustful relationship. I give good phone, by the way. He gets out of County, and we have some good times together."

Billy hadn't heard this part of the story before, and he finds it amusing. He knows his friend is compulsive, but this is just crazy, stupid lust.

"You need to take those dicky pants off, girl," he jokes.

Billy sits back while she elaborates on the fate part. She blames it all on ATT.

"It was pure fate, I tell you."

Billy listens for a while, and then he counters her story, explaining that after Miguel was released, he rejoined the crew. He made nice for awhile. No more bullshit or drama. Of course, he has a short memory. He's not even back a few weeks before he goes rogue and pulls a few jobs.

"So you can see, the mystery man is not a happy man," Billy says.

Raquel shakes her head in disbelief. Not that she doesn't believe what he is saying, she does. She shakes her head because she knows how dumb Miguel can be, at times. She's pissed off that she knew none of this.

"Okay, I get that he is stupid. I seem to have a pattern in that area. It's like that scene in *Pretty Woman*, where Julia Roberts' character tells Richard Gere's character that her mother dubbed her a loser magnet."

Billy laughs, but Raquel isn't laughing.

"That's me," she admits. "I seem to see a picture of perfect guys that are stupid and really not that good-looking. So he did a few jobs on the side, big deal!"

"It's not that simple. It wasn't just any side job.

Miguel chose a bank he knows is off the grid, and not just any bank. This particular bank holds a discretionary slush fund for the mystery man."

"What?" she barks. "The asshole robbed the man, knowing he had money in there? What a dumb shit!"

Billy explains further that no real money was actually taken. Miguel didn't get shit, but his face was seen on the security tapes. He was out there for everyone to see. So he goes underground, under the radar. Word goes out, and now he is a marked fuck up.

"They won't just break his legs, babe," he states.

"The asshole deserves it," she says. "I can't help him, trust me. Like I keep saying, I haven't even seen him for months. Tell the mystery guy I don't know where he is."

"Do you know where he is?" Billy inquires. "You *can* tell me."

Raquel is reluctant to say, even if she knew. She has enough problems of her own right now. Billy believes that she knows, and waits for an answer. There is none forthcoming. He's seen this act before. To press her won't get them anywhere. He'll have to wait until she decides to talk, but he will leave her with some advice.

"You don't need anyone, Raquel. You use people as good as anyone. You're like a man. God, you even get off like one," he says.

She knows that he is right, but betrayal is a big

thing to her. She has been betrayed her entire life by people she thought were her family or friends. Betrayal is against the grain for her.

"I don't know, Billy. I really don't know where he is," she states.

Billy believes her, but offers more advice. "They'll find him anyway, love. You might as well make some money on it."

He waits for her answer. Raquel looks away so that there is no further eye contact between them.

"You don't have to directly flip him. Just let them know when he comes around, and he will come around," he suggests.

Raquel still can't come to terms with the thought of a betrayal. Only this time, she would be the Judas.

"He will want to climb up on you. Who wouldn't?"

Raquel struggles with the thought of it. Billy can see her pain and sees the tears well up in her eyes. This sight is so not like her.

"You don't have to flip him," he reminds her. "Just . . ."

Raquel interrupts him. "I know. I heard you the first time. I can't do it, Billy. I fucking need the money, but I can't do it."

Billy understands and wraps his arm around her shoulder. "Just think about it," he says.

Enough words have been said. The rest of the flight is made in complete silent.

RAQUEL'S CAB RIDE home from Santa Monica Airport is made in major silence. She has a lot to think about. She wonders if Billy is still playing her, or if he is a true friend. Is he just a friend with benefits?

This is often her journey. She begins to doubt her own sanity or judgment when it comes to men, even if she hasn't bedded them. Trust is an issue for her. Sometimes, she isn't the most trustworthy. She keeps hearing Billy's words inside her head.

"You don't need anyone, Raquel. You use them as good as anyone."

Billy's words resonate over and over inside her head. She remembers what she's heard as a child. The truth hurts. Raquel sits quietly staring out the window, completely oblivious to the cabbie's chatter.

As the cab pulls up to her house, she realizes she left three days ago to talk to Billy and she's now just returning. Her house is dark and it seems so distant to her. Raquel pays the cabbie and gets out. In seconds, he pulls away. She stands there, staring at her house, and instantly sees a flashing light pass through her living room.

"What the fuck?" she says to herself. "Has Billy already thrown me under the fucking bus?"

The cabbie is already gone, so she's on her own. She stands at the curb, watching the flashing lights move through her house. Raquel decides to go around the back to get a better advantage point. She keeps to the side of the house, concealed by the shadows, waiting to see who might come out.

She has no fear. She's curious as to who the person moving through her home might be since no one really knows where she is living. Voices soon reach her, and she slides back into the shadows.

The intruder steps out the front door, talking on the phone. "She's not here," he reports. "No, I went to the Chateau Marmont. Billy's not there. They said he was out of town on some gig."

He hangs up the phone and heads for the street. Raquel watches from her hiding place as he crosses the street, gets into his dark unmarked car, and drives away. She waits until he is gone before she moves toward the house.

Once inside, she sees a few things thrown around, but there's no real damage done. They are looking for Miguel, and the most obvious place would be her home.

Raquel doesn't bother to turn the lights on. Why draw attention or let them know that she is home? She walks to the refrigerator and pulls out a beer. Making her way to the kitchen table, she sits down to think. She wonders if it's best to get out of town for a while. Her friend, Alexa, has been bugging her to take a ride to Susanville to visit her boyfriend in prison. She takes a sip of her drink and stares into the darkness. A smile soon appears on her face.

"Time for this girl to take a week's vacation and get out of town!" she affirms. "Time to hit the fucking road!"

3

SUSANVILLE (formerly, Rooptown) is the county seat of Lassen County, California. Susanville is located on the Susan River in the southern part of the county. The city, a former logging and mining town, is the site of the High Desert State Prison and the California Correctional Center. High Desert State Prison, a maximum-security facility, opened in 1995. The California Correctional Center, a minimum-medium security facility, opened in 1963.

Raquel and Alexa put Los Angeles behind them, and make the long drive north to Susanville, only to find out that no passes are being allowed. Alexa argues that they have come a long way, but the officer in charge turns a deaf ear, and they are turned away without explanation.

"There will be no visiting today or any other day," he reports.

Raquel doesn't like the manner in which he delivers the message, so she delivers one of her own. "Asshole, you could have told us before we made the drive."

He ignores her comment and smirks, which pisses her off even more. "Ain't life a bitch?"

Raquel wants to banter with him just for the fun of it, but Alexa doesn't want any trouble for her man.

"Come on girl. Let's go," she pleads.

Raquel hates to walk away without some satisfaction, so she flips the guard off over her shoulder as she exits. Once outside, she explodes.

"That son-of-a-bitch! I wanted to kick his ass," she rants.

"So, now what do we do?" Alexa asks.

Raquel thinks for a moment, still raging over the turn away. "We go visit Reggie."

The look on Alexa's face is priceless. "Jesus, Reggie lives in friggin' Portland, Oregon!"

"Yep, that's the guy," Raquel answers with a smile.

Alexa waits for a moment to make sure that Raquel isn't kidding around. "Let's go, then."

****

EIGHT HOURS AND THIRTY-FOUR MINUTES LATER, a very tired Raquel and Alexa arrive in Portland, Oregon. Raquel is not exactly sure where Reggie lives, and she feels uncomfortable just showing up. They decide to check into a motel and get a good night's rest. A good shower and some food is a priority at this time of night. Reggie can wait until tomorrow. Several hours later, they are sitting in the small café near the motel talking about the crazy notion they just put into play.

"I've been asking you for months to go with me to Susanville. Why now?" Alexa asks.

Raquel looks up with a smile. "I just thought it was good for some downtime," she says.

Alexa knows her better than that, and knows there is more to the story. "Come on, own it," she presses.

Raquel explains a bit of her situation without going into too much detail. She talks about her three days with Billy, and how he threw her under the bus with a mystery guy that was putting pressure on him.

Alexa reacts like a friend would. "I would have beat his ass!"

Raquel thanks her for the support, but explains that she understood Billy's dilemma and forgave him . . . this time.

"I get it. So you get time away, and at the same time, you're helping me out. You're the best," she says with a smile.

The waitress appears, ready to collect their plates. "Anything else?" she asks.

"No, we're good, thank you," Raquel answers. She looks at Alexa and offers a plan. "Let's get a drink. I'll make some calls and let Reggie know we're in town."

Alexa nods, pleased by the idea.

RAQUEL IS LYING ON THE BED, watching a bit of TV, while Alexa finishes her shower. She has made her calls and is enjoying the last of her wine when there is a knock at the door. At first, Raquel is a tad spooked. She doesn't bother to get up.

"Who is it?" she asks.

No one answers, but there is another series of knocks on the door. Raquel's concern now turns to anger.

"What the fuck!?"

She gets up and hurries to the door. Raquel hesitates for a second, and peers through the peephole. Whoever it is has put their hand over the hole. Just as she is about to open the door, Alexa steps out of the bathroom.

"Who is it?"

Raquel turns around and puts her finger to her mouth to silence her. Alexa takes a step back and waits as Raquel sneaks a peek out the window.

"Asshole!" she blurts out as she opens the door.

Standing in front of her is Reggie and several other friends. "Welcome the fuck to Portland, babe," Reggie says as he grabs her and plants a kiss on her lips.

"Let's party!" the group shouts.

****

REGGIE HAS INVITED Raquel and Alexa back to his parent's house. They are quite wealthy and spend a great deal of time away, so Reggie has the run of the house. Raquel is quietly pleased that the guard turned them away in Susanville. She hasn't seen Reggie for quite some time, and she has missed him. She has always wondered if there could have been something great with him, but he bolted early. All the same, they are good friends and their lovemaking has always been great. She knows it'll be a good week, after all.

Reggie immediately offers sanctuary to Raquel and Alexa, but Raquel declines. She feels it best that they stay at the motel. Reggie is a tad hurt by the turn down, but knowing Raquel as he does, he smiles and accepts her decision without explanation.

Unbeknownst to him, Raquel had an odd feeling when she entered his parent's house. It reminded her of her parent's house in Temecula and that feeling was enough. It's been awhile since Raquel has been home. Her father has cut ties with her during her time of chaos in order to protect his business and present family. Raquel knows this and has accepted it, since she is the one creating the chaos, but times are different now.

Reggie walks Raquel down the hallway and shoves the swinging door to the kitchen open in anticipation of some kind of sexual interlude. He senses a distance dwelling inside her.

"What's up, girl? You seem distant. Hope it's not me," he says.

Raquel smiles and immediately goes to the

refrigerator and opens it. She glances inside and pulls out some white wine.

"I've been dealing with some shit. It's not you, Reg." She walks over to him and plants a kiss on his lips. "Shall we have a private party?"

****

REGGIE AND RAQUEL spend the next three hours in his room, reacquainting themselves. The hours are filled with lust, talk, and drink. Reggie even offers party favors, but Raquel declines, which brings a confused look to his face.

"What the fuck are you doing here?" he asks abruptly.

"Nice to see you, too, asshole."

Reggie laughs at her quick retort, and then turns serious. "No, seriously, what are you doing here?"

Raquel spends the next hour telling Reggie about the last six months. He listens intently to what she has to say, and shows signs of deep concern. He wants to offer her advice or comforting words, but he also knows that unsolicited advice is not one of Raquel's favorite things.

"So, that's why I'm here," she says.

Reggie smiles and stares at her with interest. He declares that he has been thinking about coming back to Los Angeles. Raquel knows he's missed her, and although he hasn't called that much, she has never left his thoughts. If he hadn't bolted when he did, he thought they might have had something.

A smile spreads across Raquel's face. "No shit!"

"No shit," he replies.

Raquel laughs. "I thought the same thing."

For the next few hours, they discuss Reggie's return to Los Angeles and the plans they have to hook up. For the first time in a long time, Raquel feels that things are starting to turn around. The only problem is the mystery guy. She finally confesses to Reggie about the troubling situation she finds herself in, and he reacts the way she thought he would.

"We'll just deal with it," he says.

Reggie decides that perhaps it might be wise for Raquel to lay low somewhere else other than her own place for a few weeks. He suggests a beach house that his parents own in Malibu. It's quiet and secluded. At first, Raquel balks at the idea, thinking about the long drive every morning to the valley for work. She decides that since it's temporary until Reggie gets to town, it's a good idea.

Reggie and Raquel have a so-so relationship. He hates what she has done to herself, but he has his own demons to deal with. That's why he bolted. He would never judge her and knows that they are similar, in a way, and that's a good thing.

"So, hang out here for a few days, and we'll have some fun," he says.

****

A FEW DAYS HAVE GONE BY, and it's now Monday Night Football. Raquel is a huge football fan, and she's getting ready to go over to Reggie's house for a good time. Alexa has hooked up with Reggie's cousin, so she's been spending more and more time at the house. Raquel is alone at the motel and has laid out her clothes on the bed, including her favorite team jersey–the Green Bay Packers.

The sound of water running in the shower comes from the nearest bathroom before it shuts off. A wet and sexy-looking Raquel steps out of the shower and reaches for her towel, wrapping it around her. She allows her hair to fall and shakes it free, suddenly stopping mid-stroke as she listens intently. She suspects that someone might be lurking outside the bathroom door, watching her. Moving decisively, she approaches the door and pushes it closed before locking it.

"Is that you, Alexa?" she calls out.

She steps away from the door, not taking her eyes off of the doorknob. No movement or sound can be heard. She stares at the floor to see if the light under the door has changed. For a moment, she feels as if she's experienced this before.

She slowly approaches the door and presses her ear against it as she waits. All of a sudden, this confident woman experiences a panic attack. Raquel quickly moves back toward the shower and opens the door. She enters the stall and shuts the door behind her.

Raquel slides down the tiled wall to the shower floor, drawing her legs into her. *What is happening to me?* Her face shows tremendous fear as she begins to hyperventilate.

She presses her hands against her ears as she stares at the bathroom door as though she's expecting an intrusion. She begins to drift into a comatose state, and her childhood memory kicks into gear. As though it were yesterday, a picture perfect vision springs up in front of her.

****

A YOUNGER RAQUEL, aged ten or so, holds this same position in the shower. Terror has this poor girl frozen. Her knuckles are white from gripping her knees so tight. She pulls herself in tighter, listening as someone approaches the bathroom door.

Her eyes are locked on the doorknob. It begins to turn. The lock holds and it stops. Then it turns again. The door remains secure and won't open.

Raquel's eyes are streaming with tears. Fear hovers over the small body and soul. The young child shrinks into the corner of the wet shower. Her tiny body releases its fear in the form of a stream of urine, trickling down the drain.

****

RAQUEL'S VISION is soon broken. She realizes

where she is and stands, slowly coming out of her altered state of inner thoughts. Her strength and impudence begins to return. Fearless, she makes her way to the bathroom door once more.

Without hesitation, she jerks it open, ready to strike, if necessary. The room is clear in front of her. She exits the bathroom and examines the carpet to see if there are any footprints. She feels foolish dragging up old baggage from her past.

She shakes her head and sighs. "Fuck, girl, get it together!"

****

RAQUEL ARRIVES AT REGGIE'S. The party is in full swing. She pulls up and parks the car. She sits there for a moment, wondering if this is a good idea after all. Staying true to her identity and throwing caution to the wind, she laughs and gets out.

There are bodies everywhere. They are in the house, outside the house, and in back of the house by the pool. There are large TV sets in all designated areas, and the party is not wanting for food or drink.

Raquel is met at the door by Alexa, and hugs are exchanged. "I don't know why you just don't stay here," Alexa says.

"Because, I need space," she retorts.

As Raquel looks around the house, it almost reminds her of the night at the gallery, except this crowd represents all walks of life. You wouldn't find the one percent of wealthy in this country mingling with this down-to-earth group. Raquel suddenly spots a not-so-handsome face. Her hormones are immediately activated.

"Who the fuck is that meat, girlfriend?" she asks Alexa.

Alexa turns and locates her target. She frowns at the thought of telling her.

"That is off limits," she quickly adds. "He is taken. What about Reggie?"

Raquel hates the words just as fast as they come out. "Really? What a shame," she says with little sincerity. "And Reggie doesn't own me yet."

She has already locked eyes with her new conquest, and the chemistry is now in motion. Raquel plays nice, for the moment. She will reunite with the crowd, and enjoy the game and party. Her thoughts are already leaping ahead, however. Before the night ends, she knows she will bypass all common sense and integrity. She will steal the man from his woman.

****

THE GAME HAS ENDED. It has been favorable to Raquel's team. The Green Bay Packers have won, and she is ready to get nasty and fucked up. As she wanders through the house in search of her victim, she smiles and shares shots with friends. Her main objective is to avoid Reggie and cut the boyfriend from the herd.

Raquel sometimes goes out in search for love. Other times, it's all about getting laid. This is one of those times. A ten minute interlude is just fine. Then, it happens.

She spots the wandering victim, Aaron, near the poolside. His girlfriend is nowhere in sight. It's time for action because her panties are already wet. She moves toward the pool. Aaron looks up from his conversation and drink, and finds Raquel staring at him from across the pool. She lifts her beer and smiles.

It doesn't hurt the attraction that he, too, is wearing a Green Bay Packers jersey. Raquel glances at the small pool house and Aaron gets the signal. She moves in that direction. He waits, for the moment, looking around for his girlfriend.

The attraction is just as strong for him, so he has dismissed any thought of getting caught. He wants it and he's going to get it. Unbeknownst to him, the wanting and getting is not really in his hands. It belongs to the one and only—the "bad girl."

****

AARON LOOKS AROUND one last time before he enters the dark pool house. He pushes the door slightly open and looks inside.

"You in here?" he asks softly, hoping that he won't draw attention.

"Get in here and shut the door," Raquel says.

Aaron steps inside and closes the door behind him. He waits for his eyes to adjust. The party sounds are a tad muffled, but they serve as background for what is about to happen. He soon spots Raquel. She is standing behind the loveseat across from him. There is something sensual and secretive about a dark pool house, and that sets the mood for the lust about to explode. Aaron starts to undo his shirt as he moves toward the loveseat.

"Leave your shirt on," she whispers. "We don't have time for foreplay."

Aaron drops his hands from the buttons of his shirt and unzips his pants. Raquel smiles and steps out from behind the loveseat. All she is wearing is the jersey. She reaches out and he takes her hand. Raquel pulls him down behind the loveseat. As they hit the floor, Aaron is already between her legs. He buries his face against the side of her neck and bites down hard, making Raquel tremble.

"Fucking bite me again!" she commands.

Aaron bites her once more and she loves it. He makes his way down to her body, pulling up her jersey, exposing her large breasts. He can't control himself and he begins to bite her everywhere. He sucks and bites her nipples. With each bite, Raquel moans and twists. Her breathing begins to accelerate to match the pain.

He finds her wet pussy and reaches behind her ass, pulling her into his face. Aaron nips at her clit as she welcomes the inevitable. His movements are slow and then fast, bringing her closer to that beautiful moment when all her senses become one. The eruption between hers legs results in a flush of heaven squirting from inside. Arching her back, she can feel the pulsation of the pleasure, leaving her faint and dizzy.

"You're fucking nasty!" he whispers. "Like nothing I've ever had!"

Raquel can wait no longer. She reaches inside his pants and pulls his throbbing cock out, immediately opening her legs wide and thrusting it inside her.

"Fuck me, hard," she commands, and he doesn't disappoint.

As she nears climax, she hears his breath increase, knowing that he will match her ecstasy, exploding into complete rapture. Raquel digs her nails into his shoulders as she lets go. Without warning, the finale is interrupted by a huge commotion outside the pool house. The entire party is being swarmed by the FBI and local police. Aaron jumps up and panics. Raquel quickly stands and pulls her jersey back down.

"What the fuck?" he says in a panic.

"Don't panic," she tells him. "Just walk out there slowly, and don't look back like you left someone."

"What are you going to do?"

Raquel knows that she can't possibly go out there. She has no idea who is actually out there, but it's definitely the authorities and she is in violation of her parole. She left Los Angeles County, and she cannot be found here.

"Don't worry about me," she answers. "I can take care of myself."

Aaron makes sure he is presentable, and slowly exits the pool house. He closes the door behind him and is immediately confronted by the police. Raquel can barely hear him explaining to the police officer that he was just using the bathroom in the pool house since it was closer. The door opens again, and an officer steps inside to look around. Raquel is now gone.

"It's all clear here," he shouts back to his fellow officers.

He closes the door. Raquel has somehow managed to escape the small house.

****

REGGIE IS BEING QUESTIONED by the FBI about Raquel. He continues to tell them that he hasn't seen Raquel in over a year. He asks them what the raid was all about. It seems like excessive force for a Monday night football game. They are not amused.

"We had word that Raquel was at this party tonight," the FBI agent states.

"Then somebody misinformed you," Reggie counters.

"She is in violation of her parole," he threatens. "Lying to me or hiding her makes you an accomplice."

Reggie isn't shaken by his threat. "Oh, I think my

ducks are all in a row. Now, if you don't mind, you're interrupting my party."

The FBI agent doesn't like his tone, but he has no warrant and Raquel is obviously not there in plain sight. Frustrated, he instructs everyone to leave. Reggie watches them leave and glances at Aaron.

He walks over to him and whispers, "If you fucked my girl, I'll cut your balls off!"

Aaron stands there with a guilty look on his face and the scent of pussy all over him. His girlfriend comes to his side and her wrath begins. She begins to hammer him about his whereabouts for the last twenty minutes. He remains silent and takes her wrath upon him, unwilling to draw more attention to himself. Everyone at the party is enjoying the show, and it's all he can do to defend himself. He ducks her blows to the laughter of the crowd.

****

IT'S LATE NOW. The party is over and there is no sign of Raquel. Everything is quiet at the motel. There are no lights on in her motel room. The FBI has an unmarked car sitting outside waiting for her return. What refuge has Raquel found?

Raquel emerges from the shadows of the trees near the motel and spots the unmarked car. She darts back for cover. She so wants to know what happened at Reggie's, but she will have to wait for that glowing report. It's too dangerous to return or call.

She wonders who might have betrayed her this time. Was her Judas, her own friend, Reggie? *No, that's not possible,* she thinks. It wouldn't be Alexa either, though they are the only two that know she is violating her parole.

That would involve the FBI, she surmises. It has to be the mystery man. He has somehow found her. That means she has to be very careful about her movements. Or she needs to get out of town.

Raquel decides that she will head home and lay low for awhile in Malibu until Reggie arrives. Any more signs of trouble, and she is off to Mexico. The border is less than a couple hours from Los Angeles.

****

RAQUEL HAS DECIDED to go back to Reggie's to collect Alexa, and let Reggie know she is going home. She makes her way to the back door leading to the kitchen, and peeks in before opening the door. She looks for the security monitor. It's off, so she quietly opens the door and slips inside. She quietly makes her way up the back stairs to the second floor, stepping carefully to avoid being discovered.

Reaching the top floor, she turns right toward Reggie's parent's master bedroom, glancing back a couple times to make sure that no one is following her. She enters the chamber and shuts the door behind her. Once inside, she feels that she is safe. She then moves around the dark room.

Not wanting to be discovered, she doesn't turn on the lights. There is a small amount of moonlight spilling in through the massive drapes. She pulls them apart to allow more in. Raquel strides into the bathroom and turns on the light. It's an inside light, so she is confident that it will not be seen. She decides to wait for Reggie. She sees a wine bottle chilling nearby and pulls the cork, pouring a small amount in the glass and taking a much needed drink.

"Shit, that is good!" she whispers.

Now that she has found haven, she wonders what to do. She walks back into the master bedroom and sits down on the bed to think. A sound comes from the hallway. She wonders if she's been busted already. She approaches the bedroom door and listens.

"Reggie, is that you?" There is no response, so she returns to the bed and sits down. "Fuck," she silently says to herself. "I'm bored."

From Raquel's point of view, she can see a vanity table. She gets up and moves toward it, sitting down and staring at her image in the mirror.

"I'd so do me!" she says with a giggle.

****

RAQUEL PUTS HER HAIR UP as she draws the bath. She begins to brush her hair, and then sets the brush down. Picking up several perfumes and sprays, she samples them. The scent of her own mother assails her nostrils as it hits the air. She closes her eyes and tries to remember those early days. She dabs perfume behind her ear, on the inside of her wrists, and between her large breasts. It feels cool and desirable.

A strange feeling falls over her, almost evil-like. She stares into the mirror as though she is watching a voyeur watching her. Pulling the jersey over her head, she begins to sexually torment the imaginary voyeur.

This is what he always wanted and will never have, she thinks.

Raquel reaches for the spray of lightly perfumed body lotion. She sprays her palm and rubs her hands together lightly and seductively. Applying the sweet-smelling lotion to her magnificent body, she reacts with every stroke as if she were making love, performing a very sensual dance. She applies the lotion to her neck and shoulders, and her eyes close of their own volition. She massages her neck and upper chest area, and begins to quietly vocalize her pleasure.

She glances at the imaginary voyeur in the mirror and smiles, taunting him. Once again, she applies lotion to her palm, spreading it softly across her stomach. Every stroke is made with deep feeling. Raquel's torment becomes an erotic masturbation.

As she spreads the lotion, she becomes even more familiar with her own body. Her sensuous dance continues. She delicately runs her fingertips down the sides of her breasts and rib cage, softly applying the lotion to her beautiful breasts. Her back arches as she massages herself into ecstasy.

All this time, she's kept a close watch on her voyeur, waiting for a reaction. *What control he must have,* she thinks.

Raquel enjoys the ritual and continues to bring herself ever closer to orgasm. She slides her hand down over her stomach, and slips her hand between her wet lips. She gasps, her eyes opening to the pleasure as she cums over her hand, fighting back the scream of passion that clearly wants out. She relaxes and sits there, staring at herself in the mirror.

She giggles. "What do I need a man for?"

4

THE FACT THAT SHE has to go back to the City of Angels lies heavy on Raquel's mind. Although, it was nice to take a break, she knows she can't escape or run away from her problems. She's learned over the years that she needs to just face them. No matter the outcome, she's stood tall and accepted the responsibility for the actions that are set in motion by her hand.

Raquel quietly searches the house for Alexa. She needs to get home and she can't go without her. She makes her way from room to room, and finally discovers her with Reggie's cousin. She wakes her, much to her disappointment.

"Where the fuck have you been?" she whispers with discontent.

Raquel tells her that she spent the night in Reggie's parents' room and now it's time to go. She asks Alexa if Reggie is about. Alexa says that she hasn't seen him.

"Is he pissed off at me?"

Alexa shakes her head. "I don't think so. He hooked up with someone after you left."

Raquel is a tad disappointed to hear that, but then she remembers the pool house and has no complaint. If he wants to see her again, he will come to Los Angeles as planned.

She has the directions to his parent's Malibu house at the ready, and knows where the key is, so that's the plan. She rustles Alexa from the warmth of her bed, and they leave for Los Angeles.

Most of the ride home is made in silence, but along the way, Alexa opens up again and talks nonstop about her lustful night and how grateful she is that Raquel thought of the trip. Raquel, on the other hand, is remorseful that she might have screwed things up with Reggie. He is a good friend and there could be something there. She decides that she will wait and see if he will honor his intent. If not, she will go back to the valley.

****

ABOUT A WEEK LATER, just after sundown, a vehicle pulls up to a beach house in Malibu and parks next to a rental car that is already sitting out front. Jason, Reggie's cousin, steps out of the vehicle and walks to the door. He knocks, anticipating that Raquel will answer. She does and lets him in. He enters the beach house with grief written all over his face.

Jason stands, locked in a trance over her beauty.

At the same time, he knows that the message he is about to deliver will be devastating.

"Jason, what are you doing here? Where is Reggie?" she asks.

"He's not coming," he responds as he fights back the words.

Raquel is confused, but not surprised. Perhaps the pool house encounter was too much for him to handle and he changed his mind. However, she is surprised that he didn't deliver the news on his own. Why send Jason?

"He could have called. You didn't have to be the dark messenger."

Oddly, he finds himself stunned by her sexuality and beauty. Under different circumstances, he would be all over her. Raquel waits patiently for the bad news. She senses that Jason is struggling with the message.

"Spit it out, son. I've been dumped before," she claims.

Jason turns to face her, and she notices that there are tears in his eyes. Hurting someone is not fun, but tears, she thinks, are a bit over the top.

"What's wrong?"

Jason knows he can no longer hold himself back. He moves closer to her in case she needs his support.

"Reggie is dead, Raquel," he says.

The initial shock of those words is surreal, and Raquel starts to laugh. It's a silly, nervous laugh.

"That's the best you can do, you idiot?"

Jason isn't laughing. She realizes that the words are sincere. The truth is, Reggie is dead. Jason steps forward to comfort her, but she holds up her arms, indicating that she doesn't want to be touched.

"Don't!" she states.

He realizes that he is in a black widow's den, and she will spin her evil on him if he advances. Raquel is often a kind heart, but if approached without recognition or approval, she will strike to the heart.

"What happened?" she asks solemnly, still shocked by the news.

Jason spends the next hour explaining what occurred, but it is cloaked in mystery. As he details the events, Raquel's mind drifts to the mystery man. *Did my visit to Portland lead to my friend's death?* she wonders. Not hearing all the words, she looks to Jason for comfort at last and he welcomes it. She steps inside his arms, and he gladly holds her close.

"I suppose I better go home. I can't stay here," she whispers.

"No, he told me to give you this, and said that you would be hanging out here for a couple weeks." He hands her a small package.

Raquel steps back and takes the package. She stares at it for a moment and then opens it. She discovers some money and a letter. She doesn't bother to read it. Instead, she sets it down on the table and wanders to the French doors leading to the beach.

"I don't understand it. What the fuck

happened?"

"We don't know," Jason responds.

Shock settles within Raquel's system. She looks out toward the water. "How rude of me. Would you like something to drink or eat?" she asks.

"Sure, that would be great. You okay?"

Raquel nods and moves back into the kitchen.

****

SEVERAL HOURS LATER, Raquel and Jason are sitting quietly in the open doorway leading to the beach. Raquel is still lost in the thought that she might have caused Reggie's death. She wonders if she can live with those thoughts.

"He was coming down here. He told me so," he says, breaking the silence.

Raquel smiles. "I believe that with my whole heart."

She takes a sip from her wine and tears begin to form. Jason doesn't know if he should comfort her or just wait. He struggles with the emotion and Raquel knows it. She turns around slowly and stares at him with seduction written all over her face. Her eyes begin to twinkle. Her look, alone, brings his cock to attention.

"Do you want me to stay?" he asks with interest.

Normally, she wouldn't bother, especially since he hooked up with her friend, Alexa. *But it's been a week, and cock is cock,* she decides. What better way to relieve her grief than with a good poke?

Raquel takes his hand and leads him back into the house. She sits him down on the couch, leaving the doors open. She steps back a few feet and stares down at him. It makes him nervous, yet at the same time, his member begins to grow in size.

She slowly undresses. First, she removes her top, revealing her large breasts, and Jason almost explodes in his pants. She tosses it on the counter and moves forward, dropping to her knees. Jason reaches out for her, but she pushes his hands away.

"Don't touch. It's my time," she says.

Jason sits with his arms at his sides. Raquel slowly moves her hands up his thighs toward his crotch. She delicately massages his thighs, and then leans forward so that he can feel her tits pressing against his cock. He moans slightly, fighting the urge to touch her. He reaches for her once more, but she stops him yet again.

"Don't move!"

Jason pulls back and submits. Raquel uses her tits to massage his cock, and he reacts to every move she makes. She then sits back and starts to undo his belt. He watches with interest as she maneuvers herself into place. She slowly reveals his cock.

Once again, she leans forward to massage it between her tits. He screams out. Raquel grabs hold of his cock, and drives it up and down between her tits. Every stroke drives him over the edge. Never in his entire nerd life has he ever experienced anything like this. As he is settling into this magical moment, Raquel drops her mouth close to the head of his cock, and lets her saliva drip down over his shaft. She then delivers the magic.

She takes his cock into her mouth, descending all the way down to his balls, deep-throating him. He screams out as his body vibrates. Jason doesn't know how much more he can take before he explodes. Raquel doesn't want this to happen, so she stops.

She looks up at him. "Don't you dare!" she commands.

Raquel stands and drops her shorts and panties, straddling him upon the chair. She moves her breasts up into his face, and presses her feet against the inside of his thighs so that she can mount him. He wants to grab her ass, but she refuses to allow him to do so.

"Don't move, motherfucker!"

Jason freezes. He sits unarmed while Raquel rocks his world. She rides his cock with a vengeance, reaching down and rubbing her clit as she pounds at him in rhythm. Jason tilts his head back, at times, but returns to her sweaty breasts to suckle them now and again. This, Raquel will allow. He licks and sucks as she rides.

"Are you ready?" she asks as she nears her climax.

"Yes!" he screams, wanting to explode.

"Fucking give it to me, motherfucker!" she commands.

Jason lets go after several strokes, and Raquel

matches his climax. She screams out with passion as she squirts all over him. As quickly as it began, she stops and gets off his lap. She stares at him. He has been spent. He can't believe what just happened. It's gone beyond his expectations and dreams. He believes that she is the purest form of sexual evil. She's a drug and he will want more.

Raquel makes her way to the bedroom. Once she is alone, she shakes her head with the disgust she has for herself for what she's done to herself and her friend, Alexa.

Moments later, she returns to the adjacent room to a smiling Jason, feeling satisfied and happy. It's as though he has just fulfilled his fantasy. Although he wasn't really a participant, he fucked his dream girl, and who will know otherwise? He smiles and approaches Raquel, hoping to kiss her to show her his love. She, of course, pushes him back.

"We're done here," she says, her words sounding cold.

Jason feels rejected, but remembers that he has entered the web, knowing the outcome. Perhaps, he has come with the wisdom shared by his cousin. Raquel hands him a glass of wine and they toast.

"Here is to Reggie."

"To Reggie and us," he adds.

"There *is* no us," she says, cutting him short.

After sharing the toast, they step out onto the beach with a glass of wine to finish off the moment. Jason has ideas of staying overnight, but Raquel thinks differently. She wants to get to Billy to find out more about the mystery man and what might have taken place in her absence.

"How about I spend the night?" Jason suggests.

"Oh, that won't be possible," she replies. "I'm sure Alexa might be waiting for you."

Jason isn't shocked to hear the venom coming from her mouth. He is hopeful that she will not share what's happened with Alexa.

"Sure, it was great and doesn't need to leave these walls," he says with a begging voice.

Raquel doesn't respond to his words. It makes him feel insecure, but he goes with it anyway. He's a doormat and that's what they do. In time, they finish their wine, and Raquel walks him back to his car. She watches him drive away, feeling happier than when he arrived.

Why the hell not!? she thinks.

****

SEVERAL HOURS LATER, Raquel is sitting outside the beach house on the sand, staring at the lights shining along the shoreline. It's beautiful to see the bright Santa Monica lights. Raquel wishes she had the time and money to venture down there and party, but she knows that the timing is wrong. There will be time for that later. Right now, she needs to focus on three things–the mystery man, finding Miguel, and getting her kids back. Those are her priorities. She knows that her inheritance from her grandmother will help get her kids back, but that won't be possible for another ninety days or so. Until then, she can wait.

Raquel takes a sip from her wine glass and decides to wash the sex from her body in beach fashion. She jumps up, peels off the jersey, and runs out into the surf and darkness. This beach is pretty secluded. There is no real chance of shocking anyone.

She spends almost ten minutes playing in the surf. Raquel has had enough and soon returns to the beach. She raises her arms over her head and dances around in circles, utilizing the night air to dry her body. As she moves toward the house, she hears a dog barking a short distance down the beach. She hurries and slips the jersey back on, just in case there are people approaching.

Raquel picks up her glass of wine and stares in the direction of the barking. Before long, an Irish Setter appears, playing in and out of the surf as she has done before. She smiles and it grows larger when she spots the dog's owner. He is a tall and very good-looking gentleman with silver hair. As he approaches, she can see him smiling. Any apprehension she might have had is gone. The gentleman has a very athletic body and a dark tan. As he draws nearer, she wonders why she's never met this type of man before. Then again, most of her encounters are with losers. Well, almost all of them.

"Good evening," he pleasantly says. "Nice night for dip."

Raquel smirks, knowing that he got an eye full of her body. *Oh, well! Better to lay it all out there now,* she thinks. *Why not put my assets on display?*

"You have me at a disadvantage," she answers in a flirting voice. "Would you like to share a glass of wine and talk about it?"

The gentleman laughs and counters her offer. "How about I play the gracious host and invite you back to my home?"

Raquel immediately accepts his invitation. "Sure, why not? Thank you. Let me just grab a shirt and some shorts."

"Not necessary," he states. "You look comfortable and sexy."

Raquel smiles and walks over to him to join him on the walk back down the beach. As they move away from her house, she notices that the Irish Setter isn't following them.

"What about your dog?" she asks.

"Oh, Buddy? He's okay," he replies. "He owns this beach and knows his way home."

****

RAQUEL LAUGHS and is totally smitten with this gentle man. This doesn't happen to her often. She is not intimidated by men. It's usually the other way around, especially when they see all of her tattoos. He doesn't seem to be bothered by that and she likes it.

They make their way back to his beach house

about two hundred yards down the beach. They climb the protective wall and make their way across his courtyard to the back door. He checks a flower pot for his key, something she finds odd, but writes it off to being rich and wanting to protect what you have.

They enter the exclusive beach house that is elegantly designed right down to every little artifact or trinket. Raquel is impressed. This guy not only has wealth, but he also has class. He invites her to relax. He'll get some chilled glasses and wine from the wine cellar unless she prefers red.

Raquel accepts the chilled glass and white wine. He ventures off toward the kitchen, and she strolls around looking at the pictures in the house. As she nears a large table with family pictures displayed on it, she immediately realizes that he is not in any of them. She frowns and is confused. She turns to ask him about it, and is immediately struck across the face with a crushing blow that sends her into the table. She collapses to the floor.

Raquel lies on the floor, trying to catch her breath. This isn't the first time she has taken a punch, but usually it's from an angry wife or girlfriend. She can take a punch. She grew up with it. Her mother battered her pretty good as a kid, but this time is different. She has been knocked down by a man of some size. As she gets to her feet, he backhands her, sending her across the room, crashing into anything and everything in the way.

"What the fuck?" she cries, spitting out blood.

She struggles to her feet and waits for him to cross the room. He stands there smiling, showing his veneer teeth, all perfect in a row. "Who the hell are you?"

"You seemed to have fucked with the wrong guy, honey," he calmly states as he starts across the room.

Raquel looks for something to hit him with, but he is there beside her far too quickly. He grabs her by the throat and throws her, head first, into a glass case portion of the bookcase. The door shatters.

She suffers a few cuts, but nothing severe. She reaches down and grabs a large piece of the glass, waving it at him as she straightens. The gentleman steps back, looking calm and collected. He shows no fear, whatsoever, and she immediately knows that he is a professional. He is not a thug. He flashes a revolver with a silencer on it.

"Put it down, now," he commands. "If you come at me with that, you better be ready to use it."

Raquel looks at him and then at his revolver, holding her position. "What the fuck do you want with me?"

"I don't want anything," he states. "This is just a warning, that's all."

"A warning from whom?"

The Irish Setter returns to the beach house in search of its owners. This guy is not its owner. He just was using the house for their meeting. This way, Raquel is forced to leave or suffer the consequences. She has broken in and entered an expensive property.

The dog continues to bark, drawing attention from the house next door.

"I'd suggest you get out of here, Jail Bird," he warns. "I know breaking and entering is your thing, but this could put you away for good."

Raquel knows he is right, and she has no time to spare. She also knows that this guy was sent by the mystery man. How else would he know her sheet?

She drops the piece of glass and rushes out the back door, darting across the courtyard. There is no sign of anyone yet, so she is safe to get back onto the beach. She runs with all her strength to put the house in the distance. It's not easy, since she has suffered a few bruises and cuts during the battle.

****

RAQUEL RETURNS to the house. She shuts the doors and turns off the lights. She retreats to the bedroom and slides down to the floor next to the bed, pressing her back against the wall. She tries to calm her breathing and nerves. *What more could possibly happen to me?* she thinks. Maybe it's best if she just doesn't leave home; if she knew where home was.

A few hours go by. Raquel has moved to the bed, and she is now staring at the wall across from her. Her vulnerability begins to rear its ugly head. Tears form and run down her cheeks, mixing with the dry blood on her face. What she thought was going to be wonderful has turned to shit. She knows that she can turn this whole thing into self-pity, or she can suck it up and move on. She doesn't wear "victim" very well, and she isn't about to start. Raquel gets up from the bed and walks into the bathroom, turning on the shower. As the water heats, she strips her jersey off, and finds her cell phone and dials.

"Billy, it's me."

5

RAQUEL wastes no time the next morning. She sets out early for Chateau Marmont to pick up Billy. After the unexpected visit last night from the professional hire, Raquel knows that it's time to find some protection of her own. She reaches out to Billy for moral support, and if time permits, some party time. She hasn't forgotten their special time in Mexico. *Perhaps, he is ready for another long weekend,* she hopes.

She arrives in front of the hotel. Billy is already there, waiting for her. It's quite early. For a rock star to be up this early, it would have to be an act of God or at least an emergency. He looks a bit tattered from the night before. He is happy to see her again, but is a tad surprised to see her driving a rental. She pulls up and he falls into the passenger seat. He doesn't hesitate to bust her chops about it.

"A fucking rental, doll?" he jokes.

"Fuck you. It's better than the bus," she says.

Billy laughs it off. He is glad to see his friend with benefits, and wonders why she called and where they might be going. Raquel tells him that she missed him and just needed some time away to sort things out. Realizing that she can't really escape it all, she's back to deal with it. Either way, he is happy to see her and have her back.

"So, bitch, what is so urgent that you yank me from my slumber?"

Raquel looks at him and laughs. "What, you can't get off the bone for a friend?"

"Fuck, yeah," he says, laughing. "Just do a drive through. I need a coffee and lots of sugar."

Raquel laughs once more and gives him an "Amen." As she drives away from the hotel, she tells him about what happened the night before. How she returned to LA with the help of the family lawyer. She doesn't go into too much detail about her time in Temecula, but she tells him that she was attending a party at a friend's house and the Feds showed up. At first, she believed it to be about Miguel and his whereabouts, but after last night's experience, she believes that she is being tailed. That the mystery man has more of a hidden agenda than just her man, Miguel.

"I don't think so, babe," he says, interrupting.

"Why not?" she asks.

"I've been in touch with the mystery man because of my own issues," he reluctantly admits. "He asked me about your present location. I'm happy to say that I couldn't tell him anything because I didn't have any idea as to where you were."

It's the truth. She'd kept herself from telling anyone where she was.

"That's exactly why I didn't tell you."

"I know, and it was spot on," he adds. "The mystery man seems to have a real hard-on for Miguel. I agree with what you've said. That there has to be more to it than just a robbery gone wrong."

"The asshole sent a professional to visit me, Billy. The son of a bitch could have killed me last night!"

Billy is shocked and wonders if they are being followed now. He turns around to look behind them. Sure enough, there is a dark sedan about a hundred yards or so from the car they are driving in.

"Fuck, we're being tailed!"

Raquel stays calm and looks in the rearview mirror to confirm his suspicions. She starts to laugh. Billy, on the other hand, is freaking out.

"What's so fucking funny?"

Raquel glances in the rearview mirror once more. She makes a turn onto a side street just to see if they will follow. As she makes her way toward Mulholland Drive, she looks again. Sure enough, the black sedan follows. Her laughter continues, though Billy doesn't find it amusing at all.

"You keep laughing, girl. What the fuck?"

Raquel calms her friend down. "Relax. When they see where we're going, they will peel off, trust me," she confidently states.

Now, Billy is truly confused. He turns to look

behind them, and he wonders who the tail might be.

"Who you think it is? I hope it ain't that hitman dude," he frets.

Raquel laughs at her friend's panic. "It's not him, trust me. Professionals don't tail people, Billy. They set you up and come at night."

Billy remains confused and stressed, but he feels better because of her explanation. "I fucking hope you're right," he says. A light bulb moment occurs, and Billy glances at Raquel. He recalls what she's said. "What do you mean, when they see where we are going?"

Raquel smiles and chooses to remain silent.

"Where the fuck *are* we going?" he insists.

****

FIFTEEN MINUTES OR SO LATER, Raquel drives down Mulholland Drive into the valley on the north side of the ridge that separates the San Fernando Valley from Hollywood. As she makes her way toward the 134 Freeway, she glances back several times to see if their escort is still behind them. She isn't disappointed. Raquel never answers Billy's question about where they're headed, so he remains on edge. He keeps looking behind them, anticipating trouble. Raquel notices it and smiles.

"Fucking chill out," she says. "They aren't going anywhere anytime soon."

"Chill out? What the fuck? What is there to chill

out about?"

Billy goes off on a tangent about how Raquel just had her head bashed in the night before, and how she called him asking for his help. Now she wants him to chill out? To top it all off, she won't even tell him where they're headed. If she had any chance of another Mexico weekend with Billy, it's gone out the window. All the same, she sits quietly and smiles, checking the rearview mirror often, just in case.

"I'm just going to jump down here a bit onto 134, and then we'll see what they do," she states.

Raquel takes the ramp going west on 134 Freeway. She doesn't bother to speed up, hoping that the black sedan stays right behind her. Billy is totally confused, but suspects that she is taunting them and inviting the black sedan to follow.

"Are you shitting me, Raquel?" he sputters. "You want them to follow? What the fuck are you doing?"

Raquel glances at Billy and giggles. He has caught on and that makes him even more nervous. He wonders if his friend has flipped out altogether.

"Don't panic," she says. "I know what I'm doing."

Billy stares at her and then looks behind him in the hopes that the tail has peeled off, but there is no chance of that. "Okay, you better be right."

Raquel looks behind her once more and accelerates, picking up speed just to fuck with them. They respond. As she increases speed, they increase speed. As she changes lanes, they change lanes. And then, she slows down again at a constant pace.

****

FIFTEEN MINUTES LATER, Raquel exits the freeway on Canoga Boulevard in Canoga Park. As anticipated, the black sedan follows. She gets to the bottom of the off ramp and turns right. Once again, the car follows. Canoga Park is a relatively small place, so getting into the heart of it doesn't take long. As Raquel maneuvers her way over to Roscoe Boulevard, she notices that the black sedan is not so anxious to follow. They begin to slow, anticipating her next move.

"Fucking cowards," she says, laughing. She watches them closely, and they decide to continue. "Okay, bad boys, here we go!"

By this point, Billy is about to jump out of the car. He is completely uncomfortable with the whole situation. If he had known that Raquel was involving him in some chicken game, he would have never come.

"Canoga Park, bitch," he rants. "You brought us to Canoga Park?"

Raquel reveals to Billy that she shares an affiliation with Canoga Park. She has a deep past there, and it was home for awhile. She tells him how she ran with the CPA gang (Canoga Park Alabama), and that they were her people. The more she reveals, the more he wants to jump out. She explains that she once took a strike for another CPA member, since he had two strikes already and a third would send him away for good.

"You fucking what!?" he yells.

"No big deal," she casually says. "I did what was considered "good" in street politics. I would have done the same for you."

"You're fucking nuts! So what are we doing here?"

She turns onto Roscoe Boulevard. Not that far down, hidden behind a used car lot, they find the Golden Cadillac Bar. Raquel pulls in and stops. There is a banner above the door with the "3" washed up middle-aged hags lying on a pool table with some scandalous lookin' ass fool. Raquel was never sure if this banner was supposed to portray what sort of events take place in this bar, or if it just hasn't been taken down since its inception.

"I only found it because I yelped the taco joint next door," she states. "I came here on a whim one night, since it's right around the corner from my god-forsaken crib, and realized that a friend of one of my friends bartends here."

Billy is speechless. He sits there, staring at her with complete disbelief. He looks behind them and spots the black sedan down the street on the opposite side of Roscoe.

"Well, I guess you were right," he says. "Those stupid fucks ain't coming over here."

Raquel laughs. "Told you so!"

"Okay, you win, but what the fuck are we doing here?" he asks.

Raquel tells Billy that she will reveal her plan after they have a drink. Now, he's a rock star, so he's probably seen it all, but stepping into this sleaze bar is not appealing to him at all. With some prompting, he gives in to Raquel's charm, and they go inside. They aren't followed, and he feels good about that.

****

ONCE INSIDE, Billy loses that comfort he was feeling. "I love a good dive as much as the next guy, but this is a good one," he jokes with sarcasm. "If it was any better, I wouldn't call it a bar at all. I'd call it a lounge."

He cautiously looks around. This place is for a low-level crowd with a full bar, TVs, darts, and pool tables in the back. The clientele, for the most part, looks like hard-drinking blue collar people you read about in books or see in movies. They are the types that drink away their last paychecks with an undiagnosed case of clinical depression.

Terrific, he thinks.

The bartender, Erin, is a cool guy and a cutie that women love to hit on. He spots Raquel right away, and his eyes light up.

"Hey, bitch, where the hell you been?" he shouts.

Raquel, feeling completely safe and at home, rolls up to the bar and jumps up, landing flat and grabbing

Erin, promptly kissing him. Billy isn't shocked by her behavior. He's shared great moments with Raquel himself.

He moves closer to the bar to make sure all the staring eyes know that he is with Raquel. He's been around the block, nationwide. This place is a typical dive, dark with a rocking jukebox. The only other time Billy felt this way was in the South, the Deep South, and that night was no fun in the end. Luckily for him, the place is quite empty. Billy looks around while Raquel massages Erin's body. He spots another better lit room with a pool table in the back. He's starting to relax until he hears Erin and Raquel speaking in hushed tones.

"Fucking cops were in about a month ago looking for you," he states.

"And?"

"And nothing," he responds. "None of their fucking business."

Billy, feeling left out, steps up to the bar and tries to make a joke. "It looks like you have a few people pissing away their General Relief check."

Raquel finds what he says appalling and berates him. "Shut up, Billy!"

Erin doesn't take offense at all and throws in some humor. "This is the kind of place where you can get your throat cut, and the cop investigating will ask you, 'Well, what did you expect?'"

Raquel appreciates his humor and for not taking offense. She laughs. Billy loosens up and laughs with her.

"That's all I was saying!" Billy says, happy that he is off the hook.

He looks around to make sure that there isn't anyone behind him about to cut his throat because of the stupid comment. Raquel grows serious and thanks Erin for his support.

"Have you seen Rob lately? I might need his help with something and would love to find him."

"You coming back to the neighborhood?" Erin asks.

"No, I can't afford that right now," she answers. "I have to stay clean and proper, or I won't get my kids back."

"I understand. I heard about your stay in County. Whatever I can do to help you get your kids back, I'm all in."

She throws herself across the bar once more, and wraps her arms around his neck. He quietly informs her that Rob is at home and she can find him there. Raquel knows the house well, since she lived there for some time. Rob does a lot of speed, more than anyone can imagine. The house he lives in is a shit show, as Raquel likes to call it. There are always people living there . . . lots of people.

It's only a three bedroom house, quite large with an office in the back that is always being used as a room as well. It's crazy living there, because the cops are always patrolling and a raid can happen at any time. That's bad enough, but there are weapons and drugs floating around 24/7.

The cops once came and thought that the dog on the premises was going to attack so they emptied two magazines in shooting the dog. How pathetic is that?

Raquel thanks Erin for the info. She and Billy set out for the house, since it isn't that far away.

****

RAQUEL PULLS UP in front of the infamous house. Billy is taken aback. He can't believe that Raquel could have ever lived there. It's exactly as she described and more. There are people everywhere, going in and out. There are even small children present. It's definitely the stereotypical drug house. They might as well hang a flashing neon light outside. *Here we are, come and get us,* comes to mind.

"I'm not going in there," Billy says.

"Okay. Stay out here, unprotected," she answers abruptly.

Billy immediately changes his tune and follows her inside. He looks behind them, and to his surprise, the black sedan is nowhere in sight. Maybe that's not a good thing.

Raquel enters the house as if she owns the place. She receives all of the appropriate salutations from everyone that either knows her or has heard about her. She smiles and feels wanted. Billy, on the other hand, feels like a third wheel and would love to be invisible. They work their way to the back office in search of Rob. As they move through the dark dingy place, Billy stays close to Raquel.

"I'm going to need a week of showers after this," he whispers.

"Shut the hell up, Billy," she says with resentment. "It might be by choice, but it's survival to some."

The office door is closed. Raquel stops and stares at the door. Billy is confused, but waits impatiently for her next move.

"What's wrong?"

Raquel doesn't say anything, at first. She listens, and then she cracks a small smile. "The motherfucker is getting off. We'll have to wait."

Billy can't believe it. "What?"

A booming voice shouts from the other side of the door. "Who the fuck is out there?"

Raquel laughs and slowly shoves the door open. "It's me, Rob," she says with laughter in her voice.

As they enter the office, they find Rob sitting in a black leather high back chair, completely naked, working on the computer. Tattoos run up and down his back.

Rob stares past Raquel at Billy. "What the fuck?" he says. "Welcome home, bitch. Who's the baggage?"

Though Billy thinks he's experienced some crazy shit before, this is not the case. He forces his laughter into submission, hoping he won't get pummeled.

"I thought I was a crazy fuck!" he whispers.

"You are, you dumb fuck. Shut up," she says

98

without turning around. "Rob, have you seen Miguel?"

"Hang on." Rob adjusts his position in his chair, and takes another hard look at Billy. "No, haven't seen the fuck up. I heard about his shit, though. You still messin' with that fucking moron?"

"No, not lately, but I need to find him. I'm getting a bit of grief from someone. I can't sort it out until I find him."

Rob doesn't like the sound of that. He gestures at Raquel, wanting her to come closer, and holds up his hand when Billy tries to follow.

He glares at Raquel. "What motherfucker is messin' with my people?" he asks with concern.

Raquel takes a moment to explain the last few months of her life. He listens with interest to every word spoken. When she mentions the mystery man, a concerned look spreads across his face. He asks several questions relating to that night at the gallery, and Raquel tells him exactly what was said and offered. He knows the loyalty she possesses and he respects her for it, but he wonders if she might just make an exception in Miguel's case.

"He's a fuck up, girl," he states. "Maybe you should consider the offer."

Raquel has been hearing that a lot lately, but she can't make an exception to principle. Even though Miguel is what he says he is, she just can't do it. He is family, of sorts. She shakes her head. He accepts her principle, and again, respects her for it.

"What do you need from me, baby?" he asks.

Raquel continues to tell her story about the professional sent to the beach house to warn her. She would like the CPA to have her back in case some bad shit comes down. Rob doesn't say a word. He nods instead. That is his word, his bond. Raquel thanks him for his time, and she turns to leave.

"I heard that Miguel might be held up at Barker Ranch," he offers.

"Thank you," Raquel says with a smile.

The whole time this conversation has been going on, Billy has been standing there in shock. He's speechless. Though he's heard stories about the antics and craziness of rock stars, and he's patterned his own career around the very thought, hoping to emulate them, he's never seen anything like this throughout his young life. Mind-blown, he meagerly follows Raquel out.

****

AS RAQUEL TURNS back onto Roscoe Boulevard, she makes her way toward the freeway. They see that the black sedan along the roadside surrounded by CPA members. It appears that the ride home will be less stressful. Billy can't help but to stare as they go by. Raquel smiles and stares straight ahead.

"He didn't waste any time, that Rob dude."

"Nope," she says, and hits the accelerator.

RAQUEL ARRIVES back at Chateau Marmont to drop Billy off. He quietly gets out. Before he closes the door, he looks down at his friend with a sad look on his face.

"I love you, I do, but I think we should take a break for a bit," he says with suppressed emotion.

"Okay, I understand. I love you, too."

Raquel knows that this whole thing is just too much for him. She can't blame him for wanting to abandon her at this time. He has a huge career to protect. Getting mixed up with her past and now her present is staring at him in the face, and it's quite overwhelming.

She knows they'll come together again someday. She's okay with that. Raquel smiles. He closes the door and walks into the hotel. She watches and waits until he disappears before allowing several tears to fall. She will miss her friend. For now, there are things to do, and she will have to go it alone.

6

IT'S BEEN A LONG DAY at the escrow office, and Raquel is tired. She heads back to Malibu during magic hour, hoping to relax with a nice bath and a chilled bottle of wine. There are still several hours left of paperwork, but escaping the valley is a must.

At first, Raquel thought it would be drag making the drive through Topanga Canyon twice a day, but it turned out to be therapy. She has too much history on that side of the mountain, and staying around could force a relapse in judgment, but not today. Raquel knows the current situation is only temporary, but for now, it's perfect.

As she pulls up to the beach house, she finds Jason sitting in his vehicle, impatiently waiting for her return. The last thing she wants to do is piss him off since he has been so supportive and was kind enough to deliver the bad news about Reggie. This is an intrusion, however, and she'll have to delicately inform him move on.

Alexa doesn't know about their encounter. She'd

rather keep it that way. Why create drama? She has enough of that already. She pulls up to the house, and steps out of the vehicle. He soon resembles a small child waiting for Disneyland to open.

"Hey, baby," he says with a huge grin on his face. "Surprise!"

"Yes, it is, and well unexpected, if you know what I mean."

He recognizes the disappointed tone in her voice. "Oh. Is this bad timing?"

The last thing she needs today is more grief, so she smiles and invites him in. He is happy and politely follows as she unlocks the door. No sooner are they inside, Jason decides he wants a kiss from her. She holds him off at arm's length.

"Jason, you need to back off, dude," she warns. "I did us both a favor by not mentioning this to Alex. Don't push your luck."

He informs Raquel that he isn't interested in Alexa and has already let her down. It was a nice time in Portland, but he is moving on. Raquel was hoping that he would beg off and go away. She rolls her eyes, thinking about beating him to death. Her image of arriving home to relax with a warm bath and a bottle of wine in solitude goes out the window.

"So, are we good then?" he asks.

Raquel refuses to back down, Alexa or no Alexa. "I'll share a glass of wine with you, but then you're history," she promises.

Jason is surprised by the brush off, especially

after the last visit. She rocked his world and now she has a disclaimer on it. Billy's words ring true once again. *"You are like a guy,"* he would say.

"So, can we explore where this is going?" he boldly asks.

Raquel is shocked by the stupidity of his statement. "No, there is no exploring, no skin time, and absolutely no future. Jason, don't make me be cruel. Out of respect for Reggie, just drink the glass of wine and say goodbye."

Raquel gives him a matter-of-fact smile and retires to the bedroom to change. Completely oblivious, like most guys can be, Jason is just happy to be there. He begins to fantasize about how gorgeous she will be when she returns, ready for play. He dances around the kitchen with anticipation, and collects two chilled glasses from the freezer.

****

AN HOUR LATER, Raquel emerges from the bedroom, looking casual, but magnificent. Jason is hot to trot. Again, she backs him down.

"Are you that stupid, boy?" she asks.

Jason is on his second glass of wine, and is more goofy than usual. She decides that it might be in her best interest to just get him drunk and send him home in a taxi, so she sets out to do just that. Over the next hour, she manages to get him pretty loaded and he is soon babbling nonsense.

"Reggie was a great guy, but I am the man for you!"

Raquel pays little attention to his babbling as she tries to complete her paperwork. Jason is so loaded that he's lost the lust between his legs. He just doesn't have the sense to get up and leave. Suddenly, he inquires about her day.

"Where were you, today? I waited a long time."

"I didn't know you were coming here today, Jason," she says in an irritated voice. "I have a job to do and weekdays are not for play. I am leaving town early tomorrow, just so you know. Not that it's any of your business."

He frowns at the thought of having to leave. Jason starts to whine a bit. She helps him have another drink.

****

OVER THE NEXT HOUR, she watches as Jason slides into an alcohol-induced oblivion and is pleased with herself. He's now completely passed out. Her earlier wish is about to come true. She will have total solitude in about thirty minutes.

The taxi arrives on time and collects Jason. Raquel gives the driver instructions to take Jason wherever he wishes to go. The taxi driver is stunned, but happy to do so. She rifles through Jason's wallet and hands the taxi driver three hundred and fifty dollars. It isn't long before the taxi pulls away with a very drunk and passed out passenger sitting in the back seat.

Raquel enters the house once more. She pulls a fresh chilled glass from the freezer, and pours some wine into it before she walks out onto the beach. She sits down and begins to reminisce about the day, feeling sad about how it ended with Billy.

She knows they will come together in the near future. It's always been that way with them. She almost expects it, but for some reason, today seems different. It's as though he was afraid of her in some way. Perhaps he's afraid of what could happen if he continues to hang out with her.

Raquel shakes her head, hoping to clear her thoughts, and walks out to the surf with her glass in hand. She takes a deep breath and walks into the breaking waves. The sound of an Irish Setter barking reaches her ears. She quickly turns her attention to the left to see if she is about to experience episode two or death. Panic sets in and she runs toward the house, glancing back at the dark beach every so often. The Irish Setter pierces the darkness, happily running up to her, dancing around her. She looks around, but there is no one in sight.

"You got out again," she says. "You bad boy! You need to go home."

The dog continues to play, and she is happy for the company. She goes back to the surf and he follows. *This could not have come at a better time,* she thinks. She plays in the surf with the dog for a bit before he darts off into the darkness, back the way he came, and everything is silent once more.

Raquel smiles and walks back to the beach house. As she steps inside, her sixth sense kicks in and she feels that someone has entered her space. She slowly looks around and wonders if she has fallen victim once again. Perhaps this might be the last time.

She moves slowly toward the fireplace to retrieve the poker for protection. The sight of an intruder lurking in the shadows of the room catches her by surprise. She starts to scream, but doesn't, for some unknown reason. The distinguished gentleman, the assassin, steps out and her scream turns to anger. She decides that if she is going to die, she will go down swinging. He anticipates her move and quickly moves between her and the fireplace. She moves toward him and delivers a blow that is met halfway with a strong block.

"You bastard!" she screams! "I'll kill you if you fuck with me!"

He calmly smiles, firmly holding her wrist. "Take it easy. I'm not here for that tonight," he states. He releases her wrist, and Raquel steps back to a safe distance. "We are alike, you and I."

Raquel stares at him, waiting for his next move. She doesn't believe him and wonders how she is going to escape. He sees the uncertainty written all over her face. He's seen it so many times before in his line of work.

"Why would I come into your home this time

and not the last? Think about it."

Raquel hesitates for a moment to gather her thoughts. She realizes that what he is saying makes total sense. *Why is he here?* she wonders.

"What are you doing here, then?"

Since their last encounter, he's thought of nothing else. Doing so is out of character and unprofessional for him. It could damage his reputation.

"I watched you from a distance when you bathed in the ocean that night. I haven't been able to think of anything else since. I couldn't wait any longer to be inside you," he confesses.

Raquel stands there in shock. She hears the words, but they don't seem to register. Everything she wanted from that first night is starting to happen right now. She remembers how she fantasized making love to him as they walked down the beach. Then it all turned to hell and she found herself fighting for her life, or so she thought.

Raquel composes herself and says, "You had your chance."

The handsome assassin smiles and heads for the door. He takes about three steps before Raquel stops him.

"Wait, don't leave!" she pleads. "Stay with me."

He turns to face her. Tears are welling in her eyes. He doesn't know this side of her, but somehow it seems sincere to him. He is forced to offer his opinion anyway.

"You don't need anyone, Raquel. You use people."

She walks up to him and presses her head into his chest, wrapping her arms around him. "Maybe so, but I'm begging you to make love to me."

She kisses him passionately, something he can't resist. He curls his hands around her face, lightly biting down on her lower lip. She can't help but to want more. This is what she's wanted from the moment she met him. She slowly pulls away from him and quickly disrobes, moving toward several large cushions lying on the floor next to the fireplace.

Everything seems to move in slow motion. Raquel drops to her hands and knees, spreading her legs wide as the assassin approaches her from behind. He runs his powerful hands softly over her beautifully shaped ass. He then slowly peels off his clothing, tossing them to the side. He continues to caresses her ass, thighs, and legs. Her breathing increases with his touch. He drops his face to the small of her back, and gently runs his wet tongue over her toned flesh, causing her to let out a small cry. Raquel reaches up with one hand, grabbing her large breast and pinching her nipple. Another moan escapes her.

The assassin presses his lips to her ass, kissing and licking, making circles with his tongue. He softly parts her cheeks and drives his face and tongue into her anus, rimming her. From there, he slides his tongue in the direction of her pussy, lapping at her juices in a rapid motion.

Raquel cries out with every stroke of his tongue. He slows and hesitates for but a moment, only to drive his tongue deep into her anus once more. Her body shakes with the ecstasy he is creating as he slips his fingers inside her, working the glorious nectar to the surface as he continues to lick and penetrate her anus.

She is about to erupt. The sweet smell of her pussy, mixed with his manly sweat makes her climax. He shares that moment with a huge explosion of his own. Raquel drops face down onto the cushions, and the assassin lies on top of her. Their breathing is heavy, but slows as they submit to exhaustion.

****

HOURS LATER, the room is extremely quiet. The assassin is now dressed and preparing to leave. Raquel lies with her back to him. She is covered up to her waist, only revealing the top half of her beautiful body. He glances at her, then turns and walks out onto the beach, closing the door behind him.

Raquel lies motionless, as though she is asleep, but she is not. She is wide awake with large tears streaming down her beautiful face. She is like a chameleon, so strong, at times, yet so vulnerable. Once again, she has been abandoned.

7

AT SUNRISE, Raquel wastes no time and sets out for Barker Ranch at the edge of Death Valley. She decides that there is no reason to delay things any further. She needs answers and she can only get them from Miguel. Raquel thinks of mentioning this to Eric, her ex-husband, but he has his own issues to deal with and can be of no help to her now.

This whole adventure and this detective shit is not her bag, but the threat coming from the mystery man compels her to find the answers she needs. She wants her kids back in her life, and will do whatever is necessary to make sure that happens.

Raquel knows it isn't wise for her to go alone, so she enlists the help of two female friends. She picks up Remy, her closest friend and godmother to her kids, and Tonya, her other best friend who's known her for a very long time.

Why Remy and Tonya? Well, they both know Miguel, and they always have her back. Miguel is sure to be more receptive if the girls were to accompany her, since he knows them both as well. So, bright and early, they find themselves en route to Death Valley in Thelma and Louise style.

Barker Ranch is infamous. It's the last hideout of Charles Manson and his 'family' after the gruesome Los Angeles murder spree. It's located inside Death Valley National Park in eastern California, near a rock and boulder filled valley in the Panamint Range. It is only accessible by sandy, primitive, and rugged roads. A small one room guest house is located to the side of the main house, as well as a makeshift swimming pool (this was probably a cistern to store water in from the spring) made from cement and rock boulders toward the back of the property.

Raquel wonders why Miguel would hide himself in such a place, since the ranch is deserted now and offers nothing. *Perhaps another group has secured the premises and they're using it for a safe haven,* she thinks. Or perhaps it's more than that, and she might be walking into a war zone.

Every time Raquel leaves the house, it seems fate takes over and shit happens. The three girls are enjoying the time away together. It's been awhile since they've done so. Their busy schedules keep them apart for quite some time.

Remy and Tonya often worry about Raquel, but no matter what the circumstances are, they will always be there when she calls. Remy even sacrificed a job once so she could be there for Raquel and her kids. This is what friends do without judgment. Or at least, that's what friends are supposed to do.

In Raquel's case, the opposite has always occurred. She gets screwed over or abandoned. She'll tell you that it's karma for all the bad shit she dealt out in her early years. *It always comes back to haunt me*, she thinks.

Remy and Tonya have a different take on it. "It's bullshit!" they chime in together.

Remy is Raquel's reality check. She lets her know when she is fucking up. Raquel can deal with that, but there was a time when they weren't so close. Words like "hate" and "despise" were thrown back and forth between them.

Both met when they occupied apartments in Tarzana on Collins Street. Remy and her friend, Caitlyn, were loud and disorderly. At the time, Raquel's kids were quite young. She'd recently moved there and was trying to settle in with her kids.

Remy's loud and outrageous personality was too much to handle at 2:00 AM. They aren't sure when it actually happened, but they became friends. Through the years, they've leaned on one another for just about everything. Granted, disagreements have occurred over the years, but the love they share is unbreakable.

Amen.

****

AS THEY MAKE THEIR WAY up the 14 Freeway

toward Palmdale, Raquel explains to her friends what has happened since she was released from the Twin Towers. Each friend knows only pieces of the puzzle, but they've never had the opportunity to discuss the details. Raquel talks about the first night and how Billy delivered her to the mystery man in order to avoid IRS issues.

"Motherfucker!" Remy shouts. "I hope you busted his skinny ass!"

Raquel laughs. "I thought about it, but I listened to what he has to say and it makes sense. There is "doubt" lurking at the back of my mind, though."

"You are too forgiving, girl," Tonya says.

"Maybe, but he has been a good friend, too," Raquel states. "I would like to give him the benefit of the doubt."

"Until he fucks up again," Remy interjects.

They laugh. Remy is curious about the assassin. This draws a smile upon Raquel's face.

Remy becomes a tad suspicion. "What? Don't tell me!"

"Fucked him hard last night," Raquel confesses. "Or maybe it was the other way around."

They burst into laughter once more. The two girls aren't surprised. One minute, she's immersed in hand-to-hand combat with a killer. The next minute, she's taking his hard cock and sperm like a sponge.

"You fucking cum sponge!" Tonya jokes.

"And proud of it, bitch!" Raquel says with pride amidst their uncontrollable laughter.

PANAMINT SPRINGS RESORT is on Highway 190 between Highway 395 and Death Valley, their final destination. The travel time from Los Angeles to Barker Ranch is about a four hour drive. The last part of it up to Barker Ranch has rough terrain and Jeeps are usually required.

Raquel hates dragging her friends out this far, but she needs to find Miguel, pronto! She has laid out a plan. They will get to the Panamint Springs Resort and stay overnight. The following morning, they will make the trek up to Barker Ranch.

Raquel decides to stop at Father Crowley for gas and a potty break. "It can't be far now," she says as she pumps gas.

"The ole geezer inside said about half an hour," Tonya reports.

"Okay. We check in and get cleaned up, then find something to eat."

Everyone is in agreement. They can't wait to get there.

"Thelma and Louise, that's what this is!" Remy jokes.

They break out into laughter and load up again.

****

THIRTY MILES DOWN THE ROAD, Raquel pulls into the Panamint Springs Resort. The small rustic western-style resort provides lodging, camping, and RV services. It has a restaurant and bar, and a gas station with a well-stocked general store. It is also the closest lodging near Barker Ranch.

Raquel isn't certain of the route up to Barker Ranch, so she's decided to relax and enjoy this time with her friends. Tomorrow, they will go in search of Miguel. They've already checked in and are now visiting the hospitality of the rustic bar.

Well into their second drinks, Raquel continues to tell her two friends about the night with the assassin. They are all ears. The bar is quite empty, but the young girl, maybe all of twenty-two years of age, standing behind the bar is hanging onto every word. After thirty minutes of laughing, a serious look spreads across Remy's her face, and she pops the question.

"What are you going to say to him when you see him?"

Raquel hasn't thought about it until now. She's spent so much time planning what she needs to do, that it never crossed her mind. There are things she needs to speak to Miguel about. Things he needs to clear up. Whether he'll do that is another matter entirely.

"After I kick his ass for hooking me into his business, I'll ask him about the mystery man," she says, moments later.

Curiosity spreads across the young girl's face as she stands behind the bar. She edges closer to hear the details. Panamint Springs in the middle of nowhere. When three chicks show up looking like they do and they are talking shit, it draws immediate attention. Raquel notices the girl sliding ever closer, but carries on anyway.

Why not educate the girl early? she thinks.

"Just remember, he is family, Raquel," Remy adds.

This is Remy's subtle reminder that despite what is happening, Miguel is a good guy. He is a kind idiot, but everyone likes him. It's a bit of a mystery that no one suspected him of anything other than hard work.

"Did you know that he was a fuck up?" she asks.

"Fuck yeah, we knew," Tonya says. "What woman doesn't know a man?"

The young girl behind the bar is all ears, and has stopped rubbing at the spots on the glass in hand.

"Actually, I guess I knew, too," Raquel admits. "I wondered about it, but never really inquired about it. Like Remy said, he is a good guy. There's no reason to screw that up."

Out of the blue, the young girl speaks up, much to their surprise. "If he's just a penny ante fuck up, what the hell is he doing up here with three chicks on his ass?"

Complete silence envelopes them. Everyone breaks out in uncontrollable laughter.

"Fucking A, is right, girl," Tonya says.

The young girl apologizes to Raquel for her outburst and unsolicited comment. Raquel laughs and accepts her apology.

Since the question has been proposed, Raquel

begins to summarize what has happened and why it is so important to find Miguel even if he doesn't have all the answers. The most important piece of the puzzle is to find out what connection he has to the mystery man. It can't be as simple as a bank robbery gone wrong. The others are in agreement. None of this makes sense to them. The pieces don't add up.

"Remy, Tonya, you both know Miguel. What do you think he did?"

Remy and Tonya exchange knowing looks. Remy jumps in and speaks her mind.

"I think Miguel is a great guy. A simple guy and no one you would suspect to be dangerous. I admit that, at first, I was concerned that you were jumping into a relationship too quickly, but once you decided to do it, I was on board with it. It wasn't long before I felt that he was good for you and the kids, so there was no reason to doubt your judgment, even if it isn't all that great, sometimes."

Raquel frowns, but takes it in stride. Remy has always been her barometer for men and situations. She is her Rock of Gibraltar, her reality check. Raquel professes that Remy is probably the most important person in her life, her everything. If something should happen to her, Remy would inherit the farm, including her kids.

Tonya jumps in and offers her opinion. She has always been a good friend to Raquel from an early age, but she is not so willing to offer her advice. Raquel usually has to pull it out of her, but in this case, she says exactly what's on her mind.

"Listen, when I hooked you guys up, I had no idea he would be nothing other than your normal screw," she admits. "I kind of feel responsible that you are in this position now."

Raquel offers her absolution. "Stop it, Tonya! I'm a big girl. I'm not denying that Miguel was a good screw. So swallow the guilt and just say what you want to say."

Tonya wipes away the sadness. In her mind, Miguel is a good guy. Though he was good to Raquel, she also feels something wasn't right. She has no idea or reason for it, but she is suspicious, nonetheless.

"To be honest, I don't know why I felt that way," she states. "There, I said it."

Raquel takes a moment to contemplate Tonya's words, wondering why she never said anything before. She then remembers that Tonya is not one to offer unsolicited opinion or advice. Raquel smiles and turns her attention to the young girl behind the bar.

"Anything to offer?" she jokes.

The young girl blushes and says that she has said enough already. The group bursts into laughter once more. They soon decide that it's time to rest. Raquel settles the bar tab and thanks the girl for her hospitality. She, in turn, thanks Raquel and her friends for the chat and excitement. She hopes one day her life could be as colorful.

"Don't hope for something you may not want," Remy states. "You just might get it."

THE GIRLS RETIRE to their room to clean up and get prepared for the trek up to Barker Ranch in hopes of finding Miguel and getting the needed answers. Although, it is not a four or five star hotel, the rustic resort has very clean comfortable rooms. It has all the comforts of home.

Tonya has finished her shower and is sitting on one of the queen-sized beds wrapped in a towel. She is watching the news on TV. Remy is sitting on the other bed, texting or emailing an interested party. Every now and then, she giggles and throws out a comment in response the text she's received.

Raquel is in the bathroom, just finishing up her shower. The water is no longer running, and Remy knows her turn has come. She finishes up her text and waits for Raquel to exit. She removes her outer clothes, except for her bra and panties. The door bolts open and out steps Raquel in all her glory, also wrapped in a towel. She lets her hair down and makes her way to the bed, promptly sitting down.

"Oh, I needed that," she states. "Your turn, girl."

"I'll be quick so we can get something to eat," Remy responds.

"Take your time. The water is great and quite hot."

Remy steps inside and shuts the bathroom door. Raquel decides to check her emails and texts on her phone. She glances at Tonya, who is half asleep, watching the boring news.

"What are you watching?"

Tonya glances at her with slight confusion. "Nothing, I was half asleep. What are we doing?"

"Remy is in the shower. I'm answering a few emails. We can get something to eat soon."

"Awesome," Tonya says. "It's hot in here."

Feeling uncomfortably hot, Tonya pulls her towel away, exposing her very trim and sexy body. Tonya is of a Latin mix. Her skin is brown and quite inviting. She immediately draws Raquel's attention. Raquel tries to focus on her emails, but Tonya lying there exposed is making her inner juices stir. She exhales deeply, drawing Tonya's attention.

"What's up?" Tonya asks.

"You're what's up, girl," she abruptly answers. "You're killing me."

Tonya giggles, knowing exactly what she is referring to. She stands up and walks over to Raquel, who, in turn, stands up and tosses her phone on the bed. They stand face to face with seductive stares passing between them.

Raquel tips Tonya's chin up and kisses her. The response is reciprocated. Tonya slightly parts her lips and brushes her tongue across Raquel's own. Becoming aroused, Raquel can feel the wetness begin to cream between her legs. Tonya presses in close and they engage in passionate kissing. Sliding her right leg between Tonya's legs, Raquel can feel her wetness on her thigh.

"I want it. Right now!" she whispers so that Remy won't hear.

"Then, let's get to it!" Tonya says.

They move to the bed and lie down beside each other, still exchanging licks and kisses. Tonya guides Raquel's hand over her perky breasts and down to her stomach, pressing her lips against Raquel's. Moaning slightly, Raquel drops her hand down and slips her finger inside Tonya, rubbing over her clit. Tonya lets out a slight moan, rocking her hips back and forth, riding her finger. The faster she rubs and slides her finger in and out, the more Tonya rocks in time with it. She gets closer and closer to the edge, trembling to what is soon to be an eruption.

Their kissing intensifies. They lick, suck, bite, and tease, tasting each other until Tonya cries out in a whisper.

"Wait, I'm going to cum!" she pleads.

She slides under Raquel as she rises to her knees, taking hold of the headboard. Tonya slowly begins her tongue dance. She caresses Raquel's ass as she pushes her tongue into her pussy, drinking her juices.

"I love your taste," she whispers.

Raquel moans and rocks hard against her tongue. She cries out with every stroke. Tonya slips a finger inside Raquel as she sucks her juices, working the glorious nectar into her mouth. Raquel is just about to erupt.

"I want to cum!"

"Give it all to me, honey. Every last drop!" Tonya commands.

She increases her rhythm and Raquel matches it

with her body until she senses the electric emotion filling her. Tonya slides her hands up to Raquel's large breasts and squeezes them. Both of them are filled with ecstasy and Raquel can take no more. She forces out a full ejaculation and her sweet nectar pours down Tonya's throat. Tonya fights to capture every drop. Raquel spasms and falls onto her back next to Tonya, feeling a sense of great satisfaction.

They hear the water shut off in the shower, and scurry to get back into their unsuspecting positions before Remy comes out. Seconds later, the door opens and steam comes pouring out. Remy steps out into the room, wrapped in a towel. Her eyes narrow. Raquel and Tonya are acting quite strange, as if they are hiding something.

Remy frowns. "What no good are you two up to?"

Raquel and Tonya burst into laughter. Remy continues to frown as she steps back into the bathroom, shaking her head.

"You two are weird!" she says as she disappears.

****

THE NEXT MORNING is filled with anticipation. The girls rise early and finish breakfast. The young girl behind the bar, realizing that they are venturing up to Barker Ranch, offers them her Jeep in exchange for Raquel's rental. She's packed them some lunch and drinks. She feels a kinship with the three women now.

On their departure, she tells them that she'll look out for them at the end of the day. If they don't return by the following morning, she'll call out the cavalry. Raquel, once again, thanks her for her hospitality and new friendship. Deep inside, she hopes their trip is not in vain.

****

THOUGH BARKER RANCH is hidden in the Death Valley National Park, it's accessible through many areas. One is found through the Panamint Valley, accessible only by dirt road. Raquel maneuvers the borrowed Jeep through the rock formations with caution. Caution not only for falling rocks, but also keeping an eye out for trouble. As they make their way deeper into the formation, their anxiety begins to rise.

"I don't know, girlfriend. This might be a bad idea," Remy says.

"Too late," Raquel answers.

After a short while, they come out of the rock formations and enter the ranch. It has deteriorated some. Vandalism has taken it over, since the Manson days. Some of the structures are no longer there, including the house where they discovered Manson hiding under the sink. To their surprise, they see no signs of anyone.

Raquel pulls up to the small shack at the entrance

and stops the vehicle. "Fuck," she says with huge disappointment.

"It's a bust," Tonya replies from her perch on the backseat.

"What do we do?" Remy asks.

"I don't believe it!" Raquel murmurs. "Rob is never wrong about stuff like this." She knows he would have never mentioned it if he wasn't certain that Miguel was here. "Let's look around."

The girls make their way to the main portion of the habitat and get out of the vehicle. They walk around, looking at the dilapidated structures, wondering what it was like back in its day. They are quite young, so the Manson rage is long gone. Tonya doesn't remember it at all. Just the same, they walk through the property and structures in search of a clue.

As Remy and Tonya move around, Raquel focuses on the main structure that's still standing. As she makes her way through the building, she ventures into a side room. Something draws her attention as she looks around. Markings are scattered across the dirt floor, as if someone has recently walked there.

Raquel moves over to the portion of the floor she's discovered. Her gaze falls on a trap door. Her first thought is to open it, but doing so could come with repercussions. She calls out to Remy and Tonya. Moments later, they appear and she shares her findings.

"What do we do?" Tonya asks.

"Just call out to Miguel," Remy suggests. "If he is, in fact, down there, he'll answer."

Raquel agrees with that approach. She calls out to Miguel.

"Miguel, it's Raquel," she says. "Get your sorry ass up here!"

There is no response, and the three girls exchange looks of concern.

"Miguel, it's Remy, you dumb fuck!"

Raquel starts to laugh, surprised by her outburst. To their surprise, the trap door opens and out pops Miguel and a few of his buddies.

****

FIFTEEN MINUTES LATER, after hugs and kisses have been exchanged, Miguel introduces his friends and asks why Raquel is up there. She can't believe the questions and delivers a blow to his arm.

Miguel steps back. "What the fuck, woman?"

"What the fuck am I doing up here? I'm up here because you're a dumb fuck. You got me into something nasty, that's why I'm up here."

The look on his face is revealing. He comes to the realization that Raquel now knows he isn't working in construction and he has an alias.

"Baby, listen," he pleads.

"I don't want to listen, baby! I've been out of jail for some time now. Where the fuck you been, and why haven't I heard from you?"

Miguel admits his absence and wants to clear the air. He makes it known that he did, in fact, did do something stupid, forcing him to go under the radar. Raquel inquires about the stupid deed and asks him directly if he knows the mystery man.

"I was approached by a Fed, a mystery man, and he wants your ass," she states emphatically. "The motherfucker offered me money for your head. When I said no, he sent a freakin' assassin to my crib."

Miguel isn't surprised. He knows he'll have to own up to his mistakes. Before he has the chance to spell it out, all hell breaks loose. The FBI and the local sheriff's department, as well as the US Rangers, surround the compound. An FBI helicopter swings in overhead. Raquel, her friends, and Miguel and his friends are taken into custody.

When the dust settles, Miguel is handcuffed and led away by an FBI agent. He is placed in the backseat of an FBI Land Rover. The handcuffs are then removed from Raquel, Remy, and Tonya's wrists. They are instructed to leave the property. The others remain in custody and are forced to sit on the ground until they decide what to do with them.

Raquel's eyes fall on Miguel sitting in the backseat of the Land Rover. He's staring back at her with total confusion and distrust on his face. She knows he's wondering if she's flipped him, whether she's taken the bounty of thirty pieces of silver.

Tears shine in her eyes. She shakes her head to let him know she had nothing to do with this raid.

Like a pawn, Raquel was played and she unknowingly led the Feds to him.

As she watches the car with him inside drive away, she feels that the mystery isn't over. Miguel owned up to the fuck up, but he didn't say what it was, or what he had on the mystery man that set this all in motion. She'll have to piece it together somehow. The ride back home with her friends will be made mostly in silence, but there will be some consoling and retrospect.

The most important thing on her mind is the fact that the Feds seemed to show up at the right time. How did they know where she was going? Who could have revealed her plans? After some consideration, Raquel narrows it down to two people. It was either Rob or the assassin. She concludes that it wouldn't be Rob, but if it was the assassin, then she must have been talking in her sleep. Did she say she was leaving for Barker Ranch? She honestly can't recall.

Before any of her questions can be answered, she'll have to return to the resort and return the young girl's Jeep. It's time to go home, and that means heading back to the valley where she has more protection.

8

THE LONG FOUR HOUR ride back to Los Angeles is exactly as suspected, quiet. Raquel continues to toss the question around in her mind of who betrayed her and alerted the Feds. She should have been taken into custody for violating her parole, yet she wasn't. It's apparent that the mystery man is pulling the strings, but who is the Judas Goat? Remy and Tonya have their suspicions, but they, too, remain quiet. The silence ends and the questions rise the closer they get to Palmdale.

"So, what the fuck do we do now?" Remy asks.

Raquel hesitates, knowing it's a very sensitive question. "When we left for Panamint Springs, did either of you tell anyone where we were?"

The reaction is unanimous between Remy and Tonya. "Fuck no! How could you ask that?" they chime in.

"Sorry, I had to ask. I didn't mean to imply anything. I just need to clear that from my list."

Raquel thinks about what's happened, thus far.

She takes a moment to reveal her thoughts and plans. She feels that the assassin and/or Rob might be involved.

Remy finds that odd, except that the assassin works for the mystery man. He would be the likely prospect, although he is her strange bedfellow, so perhaps he isn't. Raquel has too much history with Rob, so that can't be possible. Perhaps there is a missing link, someone she hasn't thought of. Someone that has something to lose or is more involved with the mystery man than first reported.

"Billy, that fucking asshole!" Tonya blurts out.

"No way," Raquel counters. "Billy needed out from under the IRS leverage. He used the mystery man to his advantage, but he came clean about it, something he didn't have to do."

"Maybe he wants you to think that," Remy suggests.

Raquel refuses to believe it. In her mind, the person in question has to be related to Miguel. Perhaps it's someone close to him. Her boyfriend screwed the mystery man somehow, and that was his revenge, his payback. The fact that there is an assassin commissioned makes things far more serious than suggested.

"Who the hell hires a professional for a petty crime?" she questions.

"Miguel? What possible revenge could Miguel have for the mystery man? It doesn't make sense. He's small time," Remy points out.

"Not so fast. Maybe he's not as dumb or a fuck up like we think," Tonya surmises.

The fact that Tonya offers them an opinion catches them by surprise. Normally, Tonya is quiet and only gives advice when heavily solicited. It's almost a standing joke between them. Tonya only spills the beans in the confessional on Saturdays.

"What makes you say that?" Raquel asks.

Tonya now is excited about offering her deductive reasoning. "Well, this makes sense to me. The mystery man and Miguel are in business together somehow, and you, Raquel, coincidentally hooked up with Miguel. Fate, if you will. We know what happens when you leave the house. Shit happens. Then stupid Miguel tries to double cross the mystery man. I haven't quite figured all that out yet, though, but the dots are there. We just need to connect them. It doesn't really have anything to do with you personally. You just landed in shit like you always do because of some dumbass guy."

"As lame as that might sound, I think it's fucking brilliant!" Remy says. "The girl is right. You are part of this, whatever it is, because you fell into numbnut's bed, and numbnuts is working for the mystery man. The mystery man is in business with God-knows-who. It makes sense."

Raquel thinks about it for a moment. "It still doesn't answer the primary question."

"What's that?" Remy asks.

"What the fuck does Miguel have on the mystery

man?"

They all sit and ponder that very question. Why or what does Miguel have over the mystery man? Silence envelopes the group as Raquel returns them home.

****

REMY AND TONYA decide that they will return to the Malibu beach house with Raquel and hash out the issue. Even though they both have families waiting at home for them, this is more important.

As they roll up to the house, they sit in the car, taking in the peace that surrounds them. Exhausted, they make their way to the front door where they find a note pinned to it. Raquel pulls it down and reads it out loud.

"Raquel, I need to speak to you right away. Please call when you return. This is extremely important . . . Jason."

"What the fuck?"

"Who is Jason?" Remy asks.

"He's a stalker that doesn't understand the word no," Raquel says.

She pushes the door open. They enter, wanting nothing more than a hot shower and several glasses of wine.

****

SEVERAL HOURS LATER, the three amigos are sitting on the beach outside the house, enjoying their wine and the magic hour Malibu has to offer. They've showered and are now chilling, but there still remains the residual effect of their trip, weighing heavily on their minds.

Remy soon breaks the silence. "How the hell did you land this place?"

"Reggie arranged it," Raquel says.

The light bulbs go on.

"Whoa!" Remy begins to hum the Jaws theme. "Duunnn dunnn . . . duuuunnnn duun . . . duuunnnnnnnn dun dun dun dun dun dun dun dun dun dun dunnnnnnnnnnn dunnnn."

"Damn, girl, Reggie is a true man. I hope you didn't fuck him over," Tonya says.

Raquel tears up a bit and doesn't respond right away. The heavy drama behind the whole thing is hard to bear.

"I saw Reggie in Portland and he offered the place for sanctuary," she answers sadly.

Remy and Tonya continue to hum the Jaws theme, unaware of the fact that Reggie has met his demise. "Duunnn dunnn . . . duuuunnnn duun . . . duuunnnnnnnn dun dun dun dun dun dun dun dun dun dun dunnnnnnnnnnn dunnnn."

Raquel stops the jabbing and teasing. The conversation grows serious. "Okay, okay! You've had your fucking fun. Reggie is dead, okay? We need find out how all the dots connect."

The moment turns cold instantly. Tonya and Remy feel stupid for making fun of the situation. How could they possible know that Reggie was dead?

"What?" Tonya asks.

"His cousin, Jason, who's also the stalker, arrived last week and delivered the bad news," Raquel says.

Tonya's eyes widen with horror. "No way! What the fuck?"

"He won't be offering up any more help to me, not in this lifetime," Raquel responds with tears in her eyes.

"I know this sounds fucked up, but do you think Jason is connected to Miguel in any way? I mean, you go to Portland and fuck Reggie. He offers you this place and up pops the assassin. Then Reggie gets laid under, and Jason shows up," Tonya says.

"Maybe it wasn't the assassin, Rob, or Billy, after all. Maybe it's Judas Jason," Remy says.

"Maybe he's stalking you for a reason," Tonya adds.

Silence envelopes them as they sit with their wines in hand. Raquel breaks the solemn moment by humming the Jaws theme.

"Duunnn dunnn . . . duuuunnnn duun . . . duuunnnnnnnn dun dun dun dun dun dun dun dun dun dun dunnnnnnnnnnnnn dunnnn."

The girls burst into laughter. Together, they make a plan for Tonya to hook up with Jason and seduce him. They decide that she has to stay cool and not tip her hand in the matter. Jason is a lightweight when it comes to alcohol, so getting him drunk will be no problem. She might even get lucky and get the needed information without fucking him.

Tonya is willing to go the distance if it helps Raquel. Raquel will plan a trip to San Diego where Jason said he was staying. They'll lure him to a local sports bar, and Tonya can do her thing. That's the plan.

"Okay, then. We have a plan," Raquel says. "In the meantime, let's party tonight. Tomorrow is another day."

It dawns on Raquel that perhaps Tonya might get in trouble back home if she goes through with this plan. It's one thing to take risks personally, but to ask a friend to risk their relationship . . . well, that's different.

"Hey, girl, you sure you're okay with this? I mean, I don't want to mess you up at home."

"It's all good," she answers. "What are friends for? You need my pussy, and I'm putting it out there."

Another burst of laughter erupts throughout the room as they toast once more.

"One last thing," Raquel says. "I need to find out who really owns this house. I can't believe I didn't think of it before now. Here I am in real estate, and duh! It totally slips my mind. I'll pull the title tomorrow."

"I'll bet it ain't Reggie's parents," Remy replies.

"It doesn't really matter. I'm out of here. This is

no sanctuary," Raquel adds.

This is another piece of the puzzle to ponder. While the girls are enjoying their wine and laughter, they're unaware of the fact that the assassin is standing in the shadows behind them.

What is his agenda, tonight? Has he come to settle things for the mystery man, or is he back for Raquel's insatiable lust?

****

IT'S 2:00 AM and the house is quiet. The girls have retired to the bedroom after hours of drinking and laughter. They share the bed as they have done many times before. Raquel separates the others by taking the middle position on the bed.

She is used to this sort of sleeping arrangement. In the county jail, she was often forced to share a small space due to overcrowding. Because of this, she also sleeps with an awareness that danger is always lurking.

A small sound reverberates throughout the house. Raquel's eyes open slowly. She listens. Everything seems to be quiet, but a sixth sense tells her that they are not alone. She slowly slides down to the end of the bed, not wanting to disturb the girls.

Raquel cautiously and slowly leaves the room, moving out into the main portion of the house. Everything is as they left it when they went to bed. She looks around the room, but sees nothing until she looks to her left. Hiding in the shadows is her favorite assassin. She tenses up, unsure of what to do. To her surprise, he motions for her to follow him outside.

****

ONCE OUTSIDE, away from the girls, Raquel and the assassin walk down the deserted beach. The fog is starting to roll in, and it's a tad wet and chilly, but not enough to drive her back inside. The assassin offers her his jacket and she accepts it, wondering why he is there.

"Is this official business?" she asks.

"No," he answers. "It's personal. You need to stop pursuing this issue. You are out of it now. Stay out of it."

"I can't do that," she remarks without hesitation.

Though he knows what her answers would be, he tells her that she is in way over her head. Her past affiliation with the CPA won't help her and they can't protect her. This type of danger comes in the dead of night, instant and precise. They won't be prepared.

"I walked right into the house tonight," he says.

Raquel knows he's right about everything. She thanks him for the information, but she can't stop now. There are too many unanswered questions. She needs to know who the mystery man is and why he wants Miguel so desperately. She realizes that she is nothing but a pawn in the scheme of things, but she can't stop until she has the answers she seeks. They

137

now have Miguel in custody, so why is it necessary for the assassin to warn her?

He makes light of the fact that he is no longer in the employment of the mystery man, but that doesn't mean there isn't another lying in the weeds. She still wants to know why he is there.

"I get it. I'll take your warning to heart, but why?" she asks.

"I'm here for personal reasons," he says with a lustful twinkle in his eye.

"Oh, the assassin that can't get enough!"

He pulls her close and kisses her passionately. Raquel returns the passion. Misty weather surrounds them. She slowly drops the jacket and peels off her clothes, rushing into the cold surf. The assassin stares at her as if she's lost her mind, but his hardened manhood won't allow him to stand there a minute longer. He shrugs off his clothing and runs into the surf after her.

For the next twenty minutes, they engage in illicit sex, not unlike the first night. The weather, the rain, and the fog have no bearing on the temperature being generated between them. Raquel locks her legs around him and presses her large breasts to his chest as he enters her. It isn't long before they succumb and their orgasms take over.

****

RAQUEL QUIETLY SNEAKS back into the

beach house, hoping that her friends haven't stirred. She carries her clothes with her and drops them on the couch, moving toward the bedroom with a huge smile on her face. She slides into the bedroom and slowly moves to the bed, working her way between her two sleeping friends, pulling the blanket back over herself. She looks up at the ceiling and smiles, suppressing the giggle she has inside.

"You fucking slut!" Remy whispers, without opening her eyes.

They quietly giggle, and Raquel cuddles up to her friend.

****

THE ASSASSIN remains close to the house, making sure there is no danger lurking. The rain has begun to fall once more, and it's coming down hard now. He pulls back into the shadows and finds protection under the eves of the roof. His face soon reflects the intensity of his thoughts.

9

THE SAN DIEGO DRAMA WEEK will have to wait until Raquel deals with the reality side of her life, not that drama doesn't exist there. This week will be filled with extensive escrow work, and for the first time in a long time, Raquel will be reunited with her small children. She makes the long drive across Topanga Canyon to the valley. What is waiting for her, however, she does not expect.

Raquel usually enters the office early, ahead of everyone else, but this morning is a tad different. The owner, a real estate attorney, and his son are waiting for her. The smiles are the same, but an air of seriousness hovers above them.

"This can't be good," she says with a laugh.

The owner and his son invite her in to their office to discuss the current events and her place in the world of escrow. They compliment Raquel on her professionalism and hard work, following it up with an offer.

"Since we let Cindy go, you have excelled beyond

our expectations. We want to reward you," the owner says with praise.

"That's right! This office has been outstanding since your arrival. Even though we released Cindy and made Cruella Deville the office manager, you continued to make things work," his son adds.

Raquel laughs at the Cruella Deville reference. The new office manager has received the nickname, unbeknownst to her, of course, from the staff itself. The owners, it seems, have picked up on it.

"I'm grateful to you both for your kind words, and I truly want to accept any offer you might have, but I have to come clean about something," she confesses.

The owner and his son listen intently as Raquel tells them about her past. That she is not able to be bonded as a result of her criminal record. She hopes one day to remedy that wrong and make this a career on so many levels, and perhaps become an owner herself. After her confession, they both agree to protect her and allow her to resign with dignity. They need someone that can be bonded, and since she is not able to do so, they need to find someone who can be.

"We don't want you to leave right away, and will give you a severance package so you can get on your feet," the father says, sounding grateful.

Tears shine in Raquel's eyes as she stands. She thanks them for their kindness and agrees to search for a new place. It won't be easy leaving this office, since she has restored it to order. Although she knew in her heart this was temporary, leaving will be difficult.

****

THE REST OF THE DAY is as normal as can be until Raquel is handed a message by the receptionist. She looks at it and shakes her head. Anger rises deep inside her, but she allows it to subside. She asks for an extended lunch for personal reasons and it is granted.

Before she leaves for lunch, Raquel calls Cindy, the former office manager, to let her know that she is leaving the company. She wonders if she might have a recommendation. Cindy is happy to hear from her, and immediately offers her a job. She is now the manager of an escrow division in a new company.

"From your lips to God's ears," bursts forth from Raquel's lips. Everyone turns toward her when they hear the quote. She smiles. "Sorry, I just got some excellent news!"

****

FORTY MINUTES LATER, Raquel finds herself standing in front of a payphone at the local 7-11. She stares at the phone, knowing she has to make the call, but is unsure of what she's going to say. Throwing caution to wind and staying true to character, she dials.

142

Moments later, Gil, her soon-to-be ex-husband answers the phone. After several minutes of awkward conversation, he confesses that the kids miss her badly and they would like to see her. This brings a smile to her face.

What a day this is becoming! She has a new job on the horizon, and she will see her kids for the first time since her separation and incarceration. For a few moments, Raquel talks with her kids and tears roll down her cheeks, mirroring the pain and crying on the other side of this phone call. She knows, right then and there, that things need to change, and San Diego looms ever closer in importance.

Gil agrees to meet her at a restaurant after work to discuss the future and how she can again become part of their lives. That meeting won't be perfect, but it's a start.

****

RAQUEL ARRIVES back at the office and seeks out the owner to let him know that she has already found a new job. To his disappointment, he hands her a nice severance check and wishes her well, though she'd agreed to give him two weeks.

"That won't be necessary," he claims.

"Are you sure?"

"We might as well get used to the idea," he says.

Raquel will finish out the day, not wanting leave them with unfinished business. Tomorrow, she will start her new job. She has the rest of the week left before the San Diego trip. She might as well make some good money.

****

RAQUEL ENTERS the restaurant with great apprehension. She wants the kids back, so she will play nice until she can finalize their divorce and custody arrangements. Gil has a new girlfriend and that turns out to be a drama in itself. In the hour or so they talk, he agrees to allow her to have the kids on weekends.

If everything goes as planned, they can finalize the custody issue. Raquel is all smiles, but deep in the back of her mind, she remembers the mystery man's threat. She might work things out with the ex, but what about the safety of her children afterwards? Raquel decides that she'll have to cross the bridge once she comes to it.

****

BRIGHT AND EARLY THE NEXT DAY,
Raquel arrives at her new office. This place is a hot mess. It is a DRE escrow, which does not require a background check. Cindy tells her that they are trying to transition to DOC, which means all employees must be bonded. Raquel knows that isn't possible for her right now, and it won't last very long, but it's a

job.

Cindy explains the operation. "We have an assembly line of people," she says with authority.

One person opens orders, another draws escrow instructions, one handles payoffs and conditions, one person prepares estimated HUDs, and everything goes to funding. Raquel's job is to prepare the estimated HUDs. After funding, everything goes to Cindy to be closed out. It all seems good and streamlined, but not too far in the distant future, it all falls apart.

The Funder, Allison, was a friend of the broker. He believed she could walk on gold and could do no wrong. That whole theory went south when a file went out short, meaning that there was not enough in the file to close it. The broker, of course, has to make up the difference, and announces that everyone won't be getting their commissions for a few months until it's paid off.

Raquel suspects Allison, as do the others, but there is no proof. Eventually, she and the rest of the staff walk out because of it, but that's another story, and far down the road. Right now, she has a job, and she is preparing for San Diego. The next few days are twelve to fifteen hour days, and the money is good.

Eventually, this chapter will be behind her and she will find another job as a loan processor for a broker who wants to open an escrow division. She will make the same money without commissions, but she knows she can get a new place to live. This means that her kids will be coming home soon.

Thank God, it's Friday! It's been a long week full of surprises.

10

A FEW DAYS LATER, Raquel, Remy, and Tonya each give their excuses for another road trip, and they set out for San Diego. Raquel covers work and her probation officer. Going on a bogus business trip is an acceptable reason for leaving Los Angeles County, and it's not that far away. Raquel has friends in San Diego, so hanging out won't be a problem for a couple days.

Raquel has called ahead to organize a meet with Jason. He isn't aware of the fact that he'll be meeting up with Tonya instead. The plan is to get him to talk no matter what she has to do. Since they aren't staying at the ranch, Raquel has asked her friend, Chrissie, if they can have safe haven there. Chrissie agrees immediately, happy to see her again.

Raquel has decided that she will try to spend time with old friends, while Tonya and Remy head for The River, a popular drinking hole near the beach. If you can't get laid in The River, then you can't get laid.

REMY AND TONYA are dressed to kill and a lot

of skin is showing. They sit patiently at the bar waiting for Jason to appear. Neither of them has met him, so he will not suspect foul play. Raquel has described him and has told them that he'll have a deer in the headlights look when he enters the bar.

Sure enough, Jason enters the bar, expecting to see Raquel. Not seeing her, he thinks he's early and takes a seat near the girls, ordering a drink. He glances their way and smiles when he sees that they have taken interest in him. Not the most confident guy on the planet, he looks to his left, wondering if they are flashing on a guy behind him. Seeing that there is no one there, he looks back to find they are still looking his way. Suddenly, his confidence is boosted and he smiles. Tonya stares at him directly, letting him know that she is available. Remy remains neutral, but they put their heads together so he thinks they're talking about him. They are, of course, but not in the way he thinks.

Fifteen to twenty minutes tick by. There's no sign of Raquel, and Jason is slightly annoyed. He keeps looking at the door and checking his watch.

"Waiting for someone?" Tonya asks.

Jason smiles, embarrassed to answer. If it looks like he's been stood up, it could ruin his chances with Tonya.

"Well, it wasn't really set up. We just said we'd be here, and if the other was here, we'd have some fun."

"Maybe she got hung up," Remy says.

He glances at the door again and then decides to

slide down closer to them. "Do you mind?" he politely asks. "Can I buy you two a drink?"

Tonya looks extremely happy with the offer. She shifts her position so that she is now sitting next to Jason. "Absolutely!" she says.

Jason draws the attention of the bartender, and he comes to take their order. "The same?" he inquires.

They nod. Tonya begins her dance. Remy falls back as her friend begins to light his fire. She shoves her cleavage in his face as she whispers naughty thoughts to him. He loves it, blushing as he checks the door from time to time, hoping Raquel will soon show up. Time passes and several glasses are now stacked in front of them. Remy begins to act like she is bored and wants to leave.

She leans toward Tonya, who is all over Jason, and whispers to her. "Girlfriend, I have serious plans for tomorrow. I'm out of here. Can you get a ride?"

Jason offers to take Tonya home when the time comes. Tonya loves the idea, and kisses him unexpectedly on the mouth. He almost falls off the stool. Remy politely says her goodbyes, and thanks Jason for looking after her friend. She hugs Tonya and whispers something into her ear so that Jason thinks he's getting laid.

"Don't swallow," she whispers loud enough for him to hear.

Tonya laughs out loud and Remy exits. As soon as she is gone, Tonya moves closer to Jason, sticking her breasts in his face once more. She grabs his crotch to feel his member as it grows hard. She strokes his cock and he becomes flustered, looking around to see if anyone is watching. They all have their own game going on, so nothing is noticed.

"You want this pussy, or not?" she abruptly asks, staring deep into his eyes.

Jason can't believe his luck. No one, other than Raquel, has manhandled him sexually like this. "Damn right, I want it!" he says with a small amount of false confidence.

****

FIVE MINUTES LATER, Jason and Tonya find themselves in the backseat of his vehicle. Jason's pants are unzipped and Tonya has his hard cock in her mouth. She dances on the head and spits a few times to get it good and wet. Jason has thrown his head back, and he is moaning with every stroke.

"Give me that big cock, honey!" she demands. "I want it all. Give it to me!"

Jason loves being submissive. He can't wait to get inside her.

"Can I fuck you, baby?" he pleads.

Tonya loves his submissive nature and plays along. "Beg me, bad boy," she commands.

As he is about to open his mouth to say something, the window shatters. In the next instant, three silent shots are fired. Jason's chest and face take the hits. Blood splatters over Tonya, but she isn't hit. Shock invades her system, and she turns toward the assailant. The shadows mask his presence, preventing her from making out his identity. Panicking, she starts to scream, but he soon stops her.

"Don't scream!" he warns.

Tonya looks down. Her chest, hands, and arms are spattered with Jason's blood. The assassin instructs her to get out of the car, and make her way to the back of the bar. She immediately follows his instructions, not wanting to get hurt. She stares at the ground once she makes it to her destination, refusing to look at his face. If she doesn't see his face, she can't identify him and that makes her safe.

"You are safe with me," he calmly assures her. "I'm a friend. Believe it."

Tonya immediately knows that he is Raquel's assassin lover. "You are Raquel's friend?"

The assassin doesn't answer her question. Instead, he doles out more instructions. "Take off your clothes, all of them."

Tonya doesn't hesitate. She peels them off, standing naked before him. "Now, what?"

"Wipe your body off with this, everywhere," he says, handing her a wet towel soaked in a cleaner that will mask the DNA.

Tonya does so quickly. He then hands her another towel, and she wipes herself dry. Tonya starts to cry, and the assassin does his best to calm her nerves.

"It's okay. You're fine, Tonya," he assures her, using her name.

Tonya relaxes upon hearing her name. She knows now that he is truly a friend and Raquel's assassin.

"What do I do?"

This time, he answers. "Give me five minutes. Then go back inside, screaming out of control. Tell them that you've been robbed and sexually assaulted. By then, I'll have gone and all traces of Jason will have disappeared as well."

"But they saw me leave with him!" she says.

"That makes him the suspect. Do what I say, and you are fine. Sorry that you have to go in there without your clothes. Neither of us can afford a DNA match to Jason. Now, go!"

Tonya, still quite shaken, stands there naked. The assassin disappears. She begins to cry once more and stares at the ground. Minutes later, she moves slowly out of sight. It isn't long before her screaming is heard, echoing in every direction.

****

RAQUEL, CHRISSIE, AND REMY are in the back of the house, lying around the pool enjoying a glass of wine, laughing about Jason and Tonya.

"Oh, my God!" Remy says. "He just about squirted when she pressed up against him. Talk about deer in the headlights!"

They burst into raucous laughter. Raquel's phone soon rings. She answers and listens to what is being said. Her whole demeanor changes immediately. A look of shock spreads across her face. She holds a hand up without saying anything at first.

"What's up?" Chrissie asks.

"Fuck me. Tonya's in the emergency."

The atmosphere around them turns cold.

"We got to go!" Raquel says, and they hurry toward the door.

****

IT DOESN'T TAKE THEM LONG to get to the hospital. They find Tonya sitting on a bed in the emergency with a gown on. She isn't crying, but shows signs that she has been. She's still in shock. Raquel has brought her some clothes. Upon seeing her friends, Tonya struggles to maintain her composure. Several minutes pass before she breaks down again.

A doctor comes in and explains that she has been given a rape test. They hope to find DNA. He tells them that it will be sometime before they know if there's a good chance they'll find something since there was very little time between the rape and getting her to the hospital.

Tonya listens and keeps shaking her head. "You won't find anything!" she says.

The doctor assures them that they will do their

best. He exits the room, leaving them alone to contemplate what's happened. Raquel knows that Tonya knows more than she is letting on. She wraps her arms around her friend and whispers something in her ear.

"How do you know they won't find anything?" she whispers.

Tonya glances about to make sure no one is near enough to hear what she has to confess. Convinced that it is safe, she lets it out.

"He's dead! Jason is dead. That's how I know."

Her statement catches the others by surprise. Jason dead? The thought is far too mind-boggling to grasp.

"You killed the fucker?" Remy inquires in a low tone.

"No, you dumb shit," Tonya answers. "Raquel's lover killed him."

"What did you say?" Raquel asks, refusing to believe what she's heard.

Tonya looks around before she speaks. "Your assassin lover waited until I had Jason's cock in my mouth before he took him out. He put three bullets in his body, and I had his fucking blood all over me."

"What the fuck is going on?" Chrissie asks.

"We'll tell you later. Right now, I need you to tell me what happened, Tonya," Raquel demands.

She quietly tells them what happened after they left the bar and went to Jason's car. Raquel asks specific questions, wanting clarity about what has taken place. Why would the assassin take out Jason, and why didn't he just kill Tonya, too?

"I don't know why, but he knew my name. He assured me I wouldn't be hurt."

"What happened to Jason?"

"The assassin said it'll be cleaned. There will be no trace of him," Tonya says.

They all stand there, frozen in shock.

Raquel knows now that Jason and the mystery guy are connected. "Connecting the dots," she says to herself.

"What do we do?" Remy asks.

"First, we get Tonya released. Then we get back to Chrissie's until I can think of something," Raquel says.

"Am I in danger, Raquel?" Chrissie prods.

"No, you're not. I know this guy. He won't hurt any of us," she immediately answers. "We won't stay as planned. We'll go home tomorrow. I'll drop you guys off and I'll go visit Miguel. I need to know what the fuck he's done. I'll just ask him if he knows Reggie or Jason."

****

IT'S ABOUT ELEVEN O'CLOCK. Raquel is sitting alone out by the pool, staring at its reflection. She wonders where all of this is going. Could it jeopardize her getting her kids back?

The assassin steps out of the shadows. "You

need to bow out," he states.

Raquel is surprised, to some extent. She turns and stares at him. "What the fuck are you doing?" she asks.

"My job," he answers. "Jason was sanctioned. It's been done."

"Why?"

He refuses to give her a straight answer. "You should go back to LA. Forget the whole thing."

"I can't do that."

"You're in danger, Raquel."

She decides to drop the matter for the time being. "Thank you for the information and for not hurting Tonya."

"Welcome. I'm sorry I had to make Tonya walk into the bar without her clothes on, but I didn't have a choice. It was the only solution. I hope you understand."

Raquel fights back a smile. "The stupid bitch will be talking about it forever," she says with a giggle.

He appeals to Raquel, wanting her to go home, to forget about everything, but he knows she won't. He kisses her lightly on the lips and disappears.

The girls rise early the next morning and head back to LA. Raquel plans to drop her friends off and find out where Miguel has been taken. Tonya has recovered from the ordeal, and is already talking about walking into the bar fully naked. Her fifteen minutes of fame have arrived, and she is taking full advantage of it. Raquel is happy to see that. It lets her know that her friend is back.

11

MIGUEL IS HELD in the San Marino jail for about forty-eight hours. He is immediately transferred to the Ironwood State Prison in Blythe. Raquel finds this to be quite fucking odd. Not only that, he is processed so quickly, his sentence sends him to the same penitentiary his cousin, Eric, Raquel's ex-husband, is in.

He was processed and condemned in forty-eight hours. Somebody has to be pulling strings from a high position. I wonder who that could be, Raquel asks herself.

Raquel has been planning a trip to Blythe for some time. She needs closure with Eric. He was a good man and a good husband to her, as well as a good father to her two kids, but there is damage and accountability to be had. How ironic that this mystery leads her back to him. There are more dots to connect, and she will finally get her answers.

Raquel pulls out the title on the beach house during the week. She finds out that the beach house is owned by an international company doing business in

California. Gulf Pacific LLC, the parent company, is in Panama.

"Panama, what the fuck?" she says to herself.

She tosses the information around in her head as she heads east on the 10 Freeway toward Blythe. Raquel would have loved to have her friends with her, but she is still feeling guilty about Tonya's mishap. She thanks the Good Lord that she wasn't hurt and that she is recovering without having to submit to therapy the rest of her life. Deep inside, she knows Tonya will be all right.

During the long drive, Raquel wonders how her probation has never been an issue, especially when she was detained in Panamint Valley during the FBI raid. She wonders if the mystery man is using her and holds back the violations until he needs them. Either way, she has her own mission to take care of. A probation violation is not high on her priority list.

****

RAQUEL ARRIVES in Blythe. She makes her way to the prison and signs in. She is immediately told that it will be another day before she can visit Miguel or Eric. She questions them about that, since it states that visiting hours are daily and she knows how it works. They inform her that both inmates have been placed in solitary for misconduct for twenty-four hours. They will be released back to the population in the morning. She doesn't know if she's just being jerked off, but she has to accept the explanation. She finds a motel and decides that the best thing for her to do is to lie low and stay in for the night.

Not sure if she is safe or if she has been followed, Raquel orders takeout food and a bottle or two of wine and settles in. She finds herself wishing that her friends were with her. Alone, at night, in a strange place is intimidating. Raquel's vulnerable side, although suppressed most of the time, is rearing its head, and she is feeling abandoned. She decides that if she makes it through the night, she will be grateful.

A knock on the door startles her. She wonders what she should do. Should she hide or pretend that she isn't there? All sorts of thoughts rush through her head. She peeks out the window and sees that the maid is holding the extra towels she requested. She slowly opens the door and takes them from her, closing and locking the door behind her.

"Fucking paranoid bitch! Chill out," she says, laughing.

****

EVERYTHING GOES OFF without a hitch. Raquel's evening is quiet and without incident, something she finds unusual. In the morning, she arrives at the prison and signs in as planned. She's jerked around a bit and detained for several hours by all sorts of red tape and nonsense. Raquel is not unfamiliar with the system since she has done time.

The prison system is run by a rat race mentality, a fact she's learned quite well.

Raquel is patient and waits until they decide to grant her the visit. She requests conjugal rights with her boyfriend, though it is denied, something she expected but had to ask for anyway. Raquel needs to get him alone outside the prison population. Getting intimate with her boyfriend would have given her the answers she seeks. The one question she needs answered for herself is, who does she visit first, Eric or Miguel? She decides to see Miguel to clear the air. She needs to let him know that she didn't roll on him.

Getting through the security is fun. She is body searched by incriminating eyes and hands, though she doesn't mind. She's experienced this of her own accord. Shit happens. She is ushered into the area set aside for visitation and waits for Miguel to be brought out. No physical contact will be allowed, and there is a huge window between them. She'll have to carry out her conversation via a phone that hangs on the wall to her right.

Miguel is brought out. He stares at Raquel with anger in his eyes and heart. He still believes that she turned on him. He reaches for his phone and Raquel mirrors the action.

"If you are here to beg forgiveness, forget it, bitch," he taunts.

"Get over your fucking self, dude! I'm not here for forgiveness, but you can offer up some anytime," she retorts.

Miguel calms down. He knows that voice oh so well. Though he had no idea whether she'd go see him, he is elated to see her.

"This is the end of the line for me, babe. I'm only getting out of here in a body bag," he says with a heavy heart.

Raquel knows now that something isn't right about the whole thing. She has to know why and who is involved.

"Is Eric involved in all this?" she asks.

Miguel looks around before he answers. He never thought she'd be the one to figure things out. He stares at her for a moment.

"What do you know?"

"I know you fucked some rich guy over and he now has his foot on the back of my neck," she replies, her words coated with venom.

Miguel whispers that he never expected that to happen. Eric told him that everything was cool. Raquel's eyes flash red and she drills him for answers. He squirms in his seat as he talks about the deal and how it was family business.

"What kind of family business?"

Miguel continues to squirm and decides to clam up. He looks around, wondering if the phone is tapped, or if the guard has heard anything. Raquel is more interested in getting to the bottom of it all.

"Don't fuck around, Miguel. This is about my family. Now what has Eric got to do with this?"

"You ask your man," Miguel says. He stares at

her and hangs up the phone.

"Don't hang up, you shit!" she screams.

The guard heads in their direction, and the conversation is over. Miguel is led away. Raquel sits there, trying to piece everything together. She has one more stop to make. Eric better come clean!

****

RAQUEL HAS TO WAIT another hour before she can see her ex. There is no way she's leaving without closure on all fronts. Eric needs to hear what she has to say, and more importantly, she needs answers about the mystery and his involvement in it. After the hour is up, she makes her way back to the visiting area. Eric is waiting.

She sits down to face him. He places his hand on the window between them, and she starts to match it, but a guard restricts the motion. They sit back and stare at one another for a moment. Raquel reaches for the phone on the wall and Eric reciprocates.

"Hey, babe," she says. "How are you doing?"

"I didn't know if you would come," he answers, feeling guilty and ashamed.

Raquel can see his pain. She wants him to know that she is no longer angry.

"Eric, I want to forgive you," she confirms. "I still need to know why."

Eric nods, letting her know that he's okay. "I know, babe."

Raquel is full of questions, but she knows her time is limited so she gets to the point. "Eric, what's going on? This can't be about purses, credit cards, and shit. The Feds are all in my shit on a daily basis, it seems."

Eric wants desperately to answer, but he knows it'll be bad for him, her, and the kids, so he hesitates. "I don't know, babe. I don't know what to say."

Raquel's frustration builds. She hasn't come all this way to hear him say, 'I don't know.' She continues to press him for answers.

"Listen, Miguel is fucked, and so are you. It has nothing to do with me. I need answers from you. I stuck with you when the shit hit the fan. You lied to me. Fuck, not too long ago, you were up to no good. Our entire world collapsed when they took you away. My kids were devastated and all because you lied. You fucked us up for a long time, but I stayed loyal!"

Eric knows that she is angry. He wants to come clean, but by doing so, he could be putting her and the kids in more danger.

"I can't take that back, Raquel," he begins before he is interrupted.

"No, you can't. They harassed me for months, and my kids had to live through it. Every other motherfucking day, they were in my house, searching for nothing but bullshit and the looks and treatment I had to endure from those fucking dyke bitches with badges."

Eric sits back in his chair and stares at her. He

knows his ex-wife very well. She needs to calm down, so he waits. Sure enough, Raquel takes a deep breath, but doesn't lose her intensity toward him.

"What do you want from me?" he asks.

"I want you to tell me what is going on. Write it in fucking Braille if you have to, but tell me what is going on!" she says with conviction.

Eric thinks for a moment and looks around to see who might be listening or watching them. The two guards seem to be occupied with their conversation, so he leans in slightly, but not enough to draw attention.

"I told Miguel to stay away from them. I didn't have anything to do with it. I wouldn't because of you and the kids. I got pinched for exactly what you know already. Miguel, the dumb fuck, did this on his own bat. Now, we're all fucked. They can't do anything to me, but you need to get out. There's a journal," he whispers.

"A journal? What journal?" she asks in a low tone.

Eric starts to get frustrated. He wants to just blurt it out, but thinks better of it.

"A journal, okay?" he states. "It has names, dates, and places. Miguel hid the damn thing."

The guard interrupts him, telling him that he has five minutes. Eric waits for him to walk away, and he leans in again.

"Go back to Barker's. You'll find it there. When you find it, give it to them and this will all go away," he says before he clams up and stands.

Raquel throws out a quick question before the guard arrives. "Miguel said family business. Does this have anything to do with your dad or uncle?"

Eric shows no visible reaction, but she suspects that it does. Raquel knows she has to go back to Barker Ranch, though she will go alone this time. She watches as Eric is escorted out and her heart breaks. This man was everything to her and her kids. Deep inside, she knows he'll never see the outside world again. This is a very sad moment for her. She slowly stands and walks away.

Once Raquel is outside, she looks back toward the prison as she'd done on the day of her release. Instead of flipping it off, she starts to cry. She is lost, once again, but this time she knows where she is going.

****

RAQUEL ESTIMATES that she is about seven hours from the Panamint Springs Resort from Blythe. She decides that she will go north on 95 to the 40 Freeway and across to the 395 Freeway. That will take her to the 190 Freeway and into Panamint Springs. She never once thought of making this trip again, especially alone.

During the long drive, she checks the mirror periodically to see if she is being followed, but there are no signs of a tail. The longer she travels, the safer she feels, but she continues to anticipate the mystery of Barker Ranch. The Feds have most likely combed the area, so she wonders how she is going to find a journal.

She decides that she will try and think like Miguel. Perhaps that will lead her in the right direction. That will be a very difficult challenge. She laughs at the thought of it.

"Me, thinking like Miguel, OMG!"

****

IT ISN'T THE KIND OF DAY Raquel expected to have. She has traveled back to the Panamint Springs Resort alone. She is tired, thirsty, and unexpected by the proprietors, but welcomed, just the same. She walks into the small bar and is immediately greeted by the young girl behind the counter. She never really formally introduced herself and exchanges hugs with Raquel as she states her name.

"Kellie, my name is Kellie," she says proudly.

She is pleased to see Raquel again and inquires about her two friends. Raquel sits down at the bar and asks for a bottle of their best wine before she's willing to tell her story. Over the course of several hours, she tells Kellie how things have gone after they returned home. How Tonya goes down on some guy and he was shot by an assassin in cold blood. The young girl's eyes are open wide, and she is hanging on every word. She doesn't hesitate to "ooooooh and ahhhhhhh" from time to time. Raquel gladly reports that she is doing great, and she is over the top with her fifteen minutes of fame.

Kellie can't believe that she is back, and inquires about her revisit. "Why did you come back, then?"

"I lost a bracelet when they grabbed my wrist," she states. "That bracelet was given to me by my grandmother. It means everything to me. I'm probably wasting my time, but I have to look for it."

Kellie tells her that people hardly go up there anymore. She's confident that she'll find it. She asks Raquel if she wants some company. She and her boyfriend wouldn't mind keeping her company. She has told him so much about Raquel and her friends that he's excited to meet her.

"No, that's okay. I'd rather do it on my own, if you don't mind."

Kellie understands. "My boyfriend would like to meet you, though. Maybe we can hang out with you later?"

"Absolutely," Raquel says. "That would be great."

Kellie brings her the refreshments. Raquel thanks her, eager for some downtime and a shower. They'll meet up later that night. At the last minute, Kellie suggests that Raquel should come to her private cabin at the back of the resort. She'll have food and drinks. Raquel agrees to be there around eight o'clock on the dot.

RAQUEL FINDS HERSELF standing in front of Kellie's cabin door. She knocks and waits for the door open. Seconds later, Kellie appears, wearing very short shorts and a tank top. Her boyfriend, Brent, is standing behind her at the bar, pouring more drinks. He is wearing a casual pair of sports pants with no shirt on. He has an athletic body and has, perhaps, about 7 percent body fat.

Kellie invites Raquel in with a hug. She makes the formal introductions, and Raquel politely says hello, unable to take her eyes off of his six pack and what appears to be a very solid bulge in his pants.

Kellie notices that she is staring and laughs. "It's big," she says without hesitation.

"I can see that," Raquel responds.

Brent doesn't even bother to blush. He is totally confident in his sexuality and knows that women desire him. He hands Raquel a glass of wine and doesn't hide the fact that he's staring at her large breasts.

He smiles and states the obvious. "And I see you're packing, too."

The three of them begin to laugh. Raquel wonders if the invitation to Kellie's cabin was meant to be more than just drinks and food. The little innocent girl behind the bar is not so innocent after all. They all toast and sit down.

The room has a special aroma to it. It's one she's experienced many times. She looks around the room. This party is going to have more pleasures than just food and drink.

Kellie wastes no time. She brings out a bong and some cocaine and speed. Raquel never expected this and would normally pass since she is on probation. It could hinder her chances of getting her kids back, but for God's sake, she is in nowhere land. She consents and the party begins.

****

WITHIN AN HOUR OR SO, they are well into their party, and all clothes have been discarded. Kellie is lying on her back on the large bed, and Brent is deep inside her with his throbbing cock. Her right leg is curled around his left shoulder. He firmly holds onto her smooth thigh as he pounds into her. She enjoys taking all of him as she enjoys Raquel's sweet wetness as she hovers above her.

Raquel is facing the headboard and is on her knees, enjoying Kellie's warm wet tongue between her legs. She grabs the headboard firmly and dances to the same rhythm Kellie has set.

"You want my pussy, baby?" Raquel asks, moaning as Kellie drives her tongue up to Raquel's clit.

"You taste so sweet, and I want your pussy," Kellie begs.

Raquel turns and looks back at Brent, licking her lips, inviting him to watch his girlfriend drink her nectar. Brent increases his thrusts, focusing on

Kellie's licking and sucking, as well as Raquel's great ass as they move in unison. The girls begin to moan incessantly, begging for more.

Kellie screams and grabs Raquel's ass, driving her face deep into her pussy, sucking her juice as it pours out. Raquel responds with her own demands as she feels her lustful temperature rise.

"Fuck, that's it, baby! Lick my clit. Lick it!" she screams.

Kellie's moaning and passion increases. Her tongue dances across Raquel's lips as Brent drives hard into her pussy.

"Grab on to that ass, baby!" Raquel commands.

Kellie holds on tight to Raquel's beautiful ass as she takes Brent's driving cock. Kellie continues her assault on Raquel's lips, licking and sucking with fervor. Raquel begins to scream and moan with every stroke.

"Fuck, I'm going to cum down your throat, baby. Do you want it?" Raquel asks.

"OMG!" Kellie screams. "I want it. Give it to me!"

She sucks and licks Raquel's pussy with rapid succession. Brent increases his thrusts, driven by their passion.

Raquel screams out. "Fuck me! Fuck me!"

Kellie draws close to her orgasm. Raquel begins to talk to her.

"Do you want me to cum all over your face? I will. Do you want my juice, honey?"

She moans and submits. Raquel brings herself to climax and squirts all over Kellie's face. Kellie enjoys the erotic bath, and she wants desperately to cum. Raquel quickly spins back around and crawls down to find Brent stroking Kellie's well-shaven pussy. Raquel spits on her pussy and drives her tongue in next to Brent's large cock, driving Kellie crazy.

"OMG, I love that!" she cries. "Don't stop!"

Raquel licks her. Grabbing Brent's cock, she pulls it out and begins to suck it with interest. She slides up and down the shaft, looking up at him with inviting eyes. She takes his cock deep in her throat. He cries out. Raquel pushes his cock back inside Kellie, and Brent drives it deep. Raquel shares her pussy once again, licking his shaft and Kellie's pussy simultaneously. She repeats this several times, and Kellie draws ever closer to her orgasm.

Raquel knows that Kellie is about to explode. She begs Brent to drive harder. "Fuck her hard!" she commands. "Fuck your baby!"

Brent increases his speed and thrusts hard, dropping his head back. Kellie grabs Raquel's large breast and holds on as she explodes, squirting out around Brent's cock and all over Raquel's face. Raquel loves her sweet nectar and begins to drink it. She spins toward Kellie and offers her some of the nectar with her tongue.

Kellie rises and tells Brent to lie down. He does so and Kellie immediately mounts his face, hovering over his tongue, inviting him to lick. Raquel straddles him cowboy style, facing Kellie. Raquel takes hold of his large cock and slides it inside her, feeling his length go deep. She moans and begins to grind on it as he begins to enjoy Kellie's pussy. Kellie and Raquel look at one another and begin to kiss passionately, sucking and sharing tongues. There is very little talk at this point. Passion runs deep, forcing them into some intense fucking.

Kellie leans over Raquel's shoulder and grabs her ass with both hands. Raquel begins to pound down on Brent's cock. She presses her head against Kellie's shoulder, and begins to scream with passion as Brent increases his thrusts. His cock pushes deep inside her; sometimes slow, sometimes hard.

Raquel looks at Kellie, and slowly moves toward her mouth once again, yearning for her tongue. She licks her lips and Kellie offers her what she's been waiting for. The kiss is slow, sweet, and passionate.

She looks into Kellie's eyes. "Go down there, baby, and enjoy my ass with your man," she commands.

Kellie moves into position, and begins to lick and suck her ass as Brent drives his cock in and out. This is the finale for all three.

"You dirty girl!" Raquel moans as she watches Kellie lick her ass.

Brent can't take it any longer. He's about to cum and the girls know it. He's done his job well, and now he wants retribution.

Kellie pulls his cock out from Raquel's wet

dripping pussy. She inserts it into her mouth, driving him deep into her throat. She moves toward the tip, and he explodes in her mouth. Kellie licks and drinks until he is weak and his cock stops throbbing.

They all collapse onto the bed and enjoy the small volcanoes stirring through their bodies. For a moment, there is nothing but silence surrounding them.

"Wow!" Kellie says, feeling quite surprised. "I fucked a hot MILF."

They begin to laugh.

"MILF? I might be all of six years older than you, young lady!" Raquel objects with humor.

"You're a mom, aren't you?"

Raquel thinks about it and laughs. "Well, yes, I guess I am," she confirms.

"Then I fucked a hot MILF!"

They burst into laughter once more.

12

AFTER A LONG NIGHT of continuous insatiable sex and partying with very little sleep, Raquel, once again, borrows Kellie's Jeep and heads up to Barker Ranch. As she makes her way through the valley and rock formations, she recounts the night before that has produced a lasting smile on her face. Like most of her sexual encounters, they are spontaneous and never expected. That's when they are the most intense.

As Raquel reaches the entrance, she slows to look around before entering the main property. It seems odd to her. It's as though she has never been there, and everything is a new discovery. She rolls out onto the property and stops at the spot where they were being detained on the day of Miguel's arrest. She steps out of the car, and takes a good 360 degree look around. It's quiet with several small dust tornadoes stirring and then disappearing about the area.

"What the fuck am I doing here?" she asks herself.

She looks down at the ground, and can see all the tracks and footprints that were made on the day of the arrest. It's almost like she can see it all again. She turns to visualize the FBI Land Rover and Miguel sitting in the backseat. She can see his face, staring back at her, wondering if she flipped him.

Raquel slowly walks toward the buildings. It's apparent that things have been tossed around. She wonders if this was all for naught.

If they couldn't find the mystery journal, how can I possibly find it? she thinks.

Raquel makes her way into the building housing the hidden trap door. She finds the room again, and sure enough, the door is open. There is evidence that it has been searched. She knows that she can leave no rock unturned. She slowly descends into the belly of the tomb below.

****

AS RAQUEL DESCENDS into the dark underworld, she senses that she might not be alone. She's had that feeling once before, and she was right. She holds tight to the ladder and has second thoughts about going further. She waits and listens. Her suspicions soon go away, and she decides to continue.

She makes her way down to the bottom of the ladder, and finds herself in a cavern of tunnels leading off from the small room where she is standing. She waits as she allows her eyes to adjust to the darkness before she searches for a switch or string that might ignite illumination. The string hovers to her right. She pulls on it and a string of bulbs ignite, running through the tunnels, giving light to the belly of the underworld. The question now is, which way does she go?

Raquel looks around the small room. It's evident that it's been searched. There are footprints everywhere, and boxes and shelves have been turned. She finds a bit of humor in it all. The mess at her feet is not unlike the trunk of Miguel's car. She laughs.

"Not unlike your car, Miguel. Must run in the family!" she says with humor.

Raquel looks through the already searched material. Once she is satisfied that there is nothing there of interest, she grabs a discarded miner's hand lamp lying on the floor and switches it on to see if it works. To her surprise, it works. It'll help her make her way through the labyrinth of tunnels.

****

RAQUEL SPENDS the next hour touring the labyrinth in search of any clues. All she finds are more dark tunnels with small pockets of living quarters along the way. She wonders what these might have been used for over the years. Was it a mining town at one time, or just a way of escaping if danger was present?

Often, history documents that fortresses always

177

have ways of escaping when things weren't right. Raquel walks through the tunnels, searching as she goes, but again, she finds nothing of interest. What she does find is that the labyrinth reaches out to the entrance of the ranch near the guard shack.

Raquel exits the labyrinth into the light of day, finding that she has walked at least three hundred yards from the main building. She walks into the sun and looks back at the house. Kellie's Jeep is the only thing familiar to her. Instead of backtracking through the underworld, she decides to walk back to the Jeep from here. She switches off the miner's lamp, and sets it down near the shack, making her way back to the house.

As Raquel draws closer to the Jeep, her suspicions are realized. A shot rings out and a bullet hits the ground nearby. Raquel hesitates for about a second before she bolts for cover. As she runs for the Jeep, a series of shots ring out around her. It's odd, because although she hears the shots, the bullets strike, seconds later. This tells her that they are being fired from a distance.

Raquel reaches the Jeep, keeping herself low to the ground. She presses her back against the front tire, using the Jeep as a shield. The firing stops. Not really anticipating trouble, Raquel is angry that she didn't come prepared. She has no way of defending herself, and the buildings have been stripped clean because of the raid. If there were weapons found, they would have been confiscated.

"What the fuck am I going to do?" she whispers.

Raquel decides to try and get a fix on the sniper. She slowly moves to the back tire, and peers out around the back of the Jeep toward the hillside. Not seeing anything, she then decides to throw a decoy out to see if it draws fire. She crawls to the door and opens it, looking for something to throw. She finds a pair of boots lying on the floor in the back of the vehicle and grabs a boot. To her surprise, she also finds a bag under the front seat. She opens it to find a 38 Special wrapped in a cloth. She checks it, only to find that it's empty.

"Fuck, if it ain't my luck!"

Her eyes fall on the glove compartment. She fights her way up, staying low, not wanting to draw fire. She riffles through the glove compartment. Sure enough, there is a box of ammunition. She slinks back to the ground, and hurries to load the 38 Special.

"This evens things up a bit."

With gun and boot in hand, Raquel crawls her way to the back tire. She throws the boot out and gets ready to return fire. The boot lands. Nothing happens.

"Shit!"

Raquel realizes that her hunter is not an amateur. She wonders if it could be her very own assassin back on the job.

"Hey, okay, you got me in your fucking sights!" she shouts. "I get it, okay?"

There is nothing but silence. She wonders where

he might be. If she stays put, it's more than likely that he'll work his way down to her. She decides that she should either take cover in the main house, or take her chances and make a run for it. It dawns on her that if it was, in fact, her assassin, he wouldn't have missed. He is a professional, and even at distance, he would have nailed her.

"It can't be him, so who the fuck is it?"

Raquel decides that she'll run instead of giving whoever it is a stationary target. If she's moving, it will be difficult for him to hit from any distance. She'll wait until dusk settles so that shadows are present. Until then, she'll have to remain vigilant.

She looks around, holding the 38 Special tight. The whole point of the trip was to find the fucking journal. Now she's pinned down by some bounty hunter or scum bag. Frustrated, she decides that the journal will have to wait. Her life is more important at this point.

****

RAQUEL SITS TIGHT against the back tire as the sun moves west. The shadows are getting deep and long. There has been no attempt on the part of the hunter. She wonders if she's been sitting there for hours for nothing.

"Maybe, it was just an asshole playing around," she says, then reprimands herself. "Yeah right, you fucking idiot!"

It's time. She knows she has to make her move. Raquel moves slowly into the driver's seat, staying low. She knows that she'll only have one chance. She reaches for the ignition, but the keys are gone.

"What the fuck?" she says, panicking.

She searches the floor and sees the keys lying on the mat. She must have knocked them out of the ignition when she searched the glove compartment.

"You dumb shit."

Raquel sets the 38 Special on the passenger seat, and takes the keys in hand, slowly inserting them in the ignition. She cranks the ignition and the engine roars. Grabbing the 38 Special with her right hand, she holds onto the wheel with her left. She slides the shifter into drive and slams on the accelerator. Spinning out of control, she aims the Jeep toward the entrance and powers away. Sure enough, shots ring out in rapid succession as she darts across the property. Some hit the Jeep, others miss their mark.

As Raquel reaches the entrance, she is surprised to see that the gate has been closed and locked. She slams on the brakes. She shifts into reverse and backs the Jeep under the trees near the guard shack for cover. No shots are fired, but she knows that the sniper will soon find another vantage point.

Raquel hates the decision she is about to make. She will have to run the gate, and that means damaging Kellie's Jeep. She glances at the guard shack, and wonders if the keys to the lock on the gate are there. She then realizes that the sniper would have taken them. Her gaze falls on mailbox hanging on the outside of the shack. It is weathered and tattered, and the "A" is missing in the word, Mail.

"No, fucking way!" she says as a burst of inspiration hits her.

She slowly opens the Jeep door and slides out onto the ground with the 38 Special in hand. Carefully making her way over to the mailbox, she takes a peek inside.

"Holy shit! He put it in the mailbox, the last place they'd suspect. Fucking brilliant!"

Raquel pulls the journal out of the mailbox and hurries back to the Jeep. She jumps inside and prepares to run the gate. A dark figure stands in front of the gate. It's now past dusk. She can't see his face, but it doesn't matter. She needs to run through him.

The sniper raises his rifle and aims it at the Jeep. Raquel draws her 38 Special up to fire. Before either of them can pull the trigger, a single shot rings out. It finds it mark. The dark figure at the gate drops his rifle and falls forward. Silence soon follows.

Raquel hurries to the dead body. She turns him over. There is a direct hit to his throat. She knows she's been saved by her guardian angel, the assassin. She riffles through the sniper's pockets until she finds the gate key, hurrying to open it. She scopes the area, hoping to see her favorite assassin, but he never shows his face.

She unlocks the gate and drags the dead body to the side, returning to the Jeep. With one last glance at the main house, she knows she'll never see it again. She speeds away, leaving a cloud of dust in her wake.

Raquel knows she'll have to explain the bullet holes in Kellie's Jeep. It's not something she's looking forward to. The important thing is she has the journal. The journal sits on the passenger seat next to the 38 Special.

What a combination! she thinks. She'll have to wait until she's alone to see what's in the journal that has everyone's attention.

****

RAQUEL MAKES HER WAY back to the Panamint Springs Resort with no further complications. Taking Kellie into her confidence, she explains how the bullet holes were made in the Jeep. Kellie shrugs it off to another Raquel saga. She makes it known that Brent has several friends who work in auto body that can fix it. There's no need for Raquel to worry. There's no mention of the journal, though Raquel states that she didn't find her grandmother's bracelet, and that is heartbreaking.

After a hot shower, Raquel sits at the small bar, enjoying a glass of wine and conversation with Kellie. The County sheriff and a man in a suit that looks familiar to Raquel walk in. She remembers the man standing in the background on the day of the raid at Barker Ranch. The sheriff approaches the bar and gives his salutations to Kellie.

"Kellie, how you doing?" he asks.

"I'm good, Sheriff, thank you," she responds.

The sheriff turns his attention to Raquel while the man hovers nearby. "Good evening. You, ah, Raquel Syrah, up from LA?"

Raquel turns to face him, glancing at the man in the suit. "Yes, sir, I am."

The sheriff remains polite and starts asking Raquel about her visit. "What happened here today?"

Kellie and Raquel are confused by the question.

"What do you mean, Sheriff?" Raquel asks.

The sheriff glances at the man in the suit. "Have you visited the Barker Ranch today?"

"Yes, I have."

"Why were you up there?"

"I lost an invaluable bracelet given to me by my grandmother on my last visit." Raquel eyes the man in the suit. "He was there. Ask him!"

The sheriff disregards her jab. "I got reports earlier that shots were heard in that area. You know anything about it?"

"No, I don't."

"I'm aware of the bullet holes in Kellie's Jeep. How'd that happen?"

"They were already there from a hunting trip earlier," Kellie says.

The sheriff isn't convinced, but since Kellie seems to be covering for Raquel, there isn't much he can do. "I'll have to take a look at it later."

"Sure, Sheriff, no problem," she replies. "As

soon as Brent comes back with the Jeep, you can look to your heart's content."

Unsatisfied with their answers, the sheriff continues grilling Raquel. "I'm aware of your status in LA. Why are you up here? You're in violation of your parole."

"My grandmother's bracelet is invaluable. I took the risk for that reason alone," Raquel says. She knows he couldn't care less about her parole violation.

He hesitates for a second and delivers his last question. "Find anything else up there that's invaluable to you?"

"No, nothing but dirt and grime."

"Did you find the bracelet?" he asks.

"No, much to my disappointment, no."

The sheriff realizes that his investigation isn't going anywhere. "Thanks for your time, Kellie. Say hello to her parents for me." She nods as his eyes bore into Raquel's one last time. "I hope you enjoyed your stay. Don't come up here again," he commands. "Stay in LA where you belong." With that said, he walks away, taking the man in the suit with him.

Raquel faces Kellie once more and smiles. "Thanks for the hospitality, Sheriff. I'll think about it," she says, laughing.

Kellie laughs. "I, personally, hope you'll come back." She smiles. "But if you don't, it was great knowing you. You are one of kind."

"Likewise," Raquel responds.

13

ON THE WAY BACK to Los Angeles, Raquel lets Remy and Tonya know that she's coming back. She'd like them to meet her at the beach house. During the long ride home, she has a chance to look through the diary, and everything begins to fall into place. There are still a few blanks that have to be filled in, but she knows now that her ex-husband, Eric, is an innocent victim in all of this.

Miguel struck out on his own under the guise of family business. Most of the names on the pages and dollar amounts make no sense to Raquel, but there are some very prominent names written in this journal. Therefore, it presents a danger to many. Washington scandals don't compare to what she's found.

Raquel can't wait to share this information with her friends. She also knows that she needs to secure the journal in some way so that it doesn't fall into the wrong hands, namely, the mystery man and his cartel.

There are names in the journal that are quite

familiar to Raquel. She wonders how she is going to deal with it. The most prominent name is Eric's father and uncle, who are part of a well-known Mexican Cartel, or so she has been told.

She met the uncle once when he flew into Santa Monica airport on a private plane. She remembers going to the airport with Eric in a limousine to pick them up. The uncle was escorted by his very cold-hearted wife, who spent the entire evening staring at Raquel with evil eyes. Raquel has never been intimidated by anyone, man or woman, but for some reason, this woman made her skin crawl.

The entire evening was spent at a five star restaurant in Santa Monica. At one point, she witnessed the viper wife whispering to Eric's uncle, and overheard her saying that Raquel shouldn't be trusted, that there was no need for her to be there. The uncle waved it off, staring across the table with a smile.

"She's his wife, and that's enough for me," he whispered to his wife.

Later that night, Raquel told Eric what she saw. He waved it off as well.

"She's a fucking bitch, pardon my language. She busts his balls whenever she can," he stated.

"I don't trust her," Raquel said. "And she obviously doesn't trust or like me."

Eric told her there was nothing to worry about that night. His uncle is the man, and that is it. No woman was going to tell him how to run things. End of subject.

****

WHEN RAQUEL ARRIVES at the beach house during the late afternoon, she's not surprised to find her friends waiting for her. She hopes they haven't been waiting too long. There are happy hugs all around, and they enter the house. Raquel has a lot to tell them. They would have waited well into the night to hear the bombshell story she's about to deliver.

After twenty minutes of relaxation and getting through the first bottle of wine, they venture out onto the sand to hear Raquel's accounting of the last few days. Not wanting to lose the impact of the story, Raquel waits until they're face to face to unravel the mystery they've been facing for weeks.

As they settle into the sand and the second bottle, Remy delivers some unexpected news of her own, something she hasn't wanted to say over the phone.

"Raquel, there was a special broadcast last night."

Raquel's curiosity is piqued. "Oh?"

"Miguel escaped from Blythe," she says.

Raquel is the first to admit that she doesn't care about Miguel right now, but hearing what Remy has said and knowing what she knows now, her reaction is mixed.

"No fucking way!" she responds.

"Why do you say that?" Tonya asks.

"I went to see Eric and Miguel," she says. "Miguel is screwed. Eric told me he wasn't part of it. Told me to go back to Barker Ranch, so I did. I don't know if it's coincidence, or just plain luck, but I discovered the journal in the last place imaginable."

"Why didn't you take us with you?" Remy asks.

Raquel sighs, knowing she's missed them badly. "I wanted to, but I couldn't endanger the two of you again. I had to do this on my own. I confess I wished I'd taken you both with me, but in the end, I think it was best I went alone."

They both understand, but remind her that they're there for her, no matter what.

"You must have been lonely and bored," Tonya says.

Raquel laughs. Remy recognizes the sound she makes.

"Oh, shit! Don't tell me!" she says.

Raquel continues to laugh. A shit-eating grin spreads across her face. She dances around the topic a bit, whetting their appetites, before diving into the details of the night she spent with Brent and Kellie before she went up to the ranch. She explains how she enjoyed Kellie's company at the bar, how she'd asked about them and the fact that she was sad that they hadn't gone back with Raquel. Knowing they were missed pleases both Tonya and Remy, at least.

It isn't long before she tells them about Kellie's having invited to her to the cabin for a simple cocktail hour. She arrived as planned. When the door opened, an Adonis with a chiseled body was standing in Kellie's room, half-naked. She was invited in with open arms, and offered a glass of wine and some naughty refreshments. It wasn't long before they were on the bed and the party began. It was one of the most amazing nights she ever had, and she couldn't believe how sensual, passionate, and nasty the young Kellie had become.

"I fucking believe it," Remy says. "I saw how she looked at you when we were there the first time. I bet the bitch couldn't wait to get in your knickers."

"Damn, girl. That's crazy hot!" Tonya replies. "Give me the details."

For the next half hour, Raquel replays the entire lustful night, and how she crawled back to her room just before dawn. Remy has heard these stories so many times before, but this is a special one.

"I got to say, I'm jealous," she admits.

They laugh. The levity of the situation turns serious once more. Raquel tells them about the labyrinth of tunnels below the ranch, and how dark and gloomy it is. Before she can get farther in the story, the fog starts to roll in. They decide to make their way inside, eager to hear the rest of the story.

Once inside the comfort of the house, Raquel strikes the fireplace. They settle in close on the cushions with a new bottle of wine, Raquel begins with the rest of her story. She recalls how she ventured through the underworld trying to find the journal, and how frustrated she was to come up empty-handed. She explains how the tunnel led back to the entrance. How once she was outside, she decided to make her way back to the Jeep instead of going back through the labyrinth.

"Makes sense to me," Tonya says.

"That's when all hell broke loose. I was dancing around with bullets flying left and right. I almost peed myself as I raced for cover. Everything went quiet again when I reached the Jeep."

"Who the fuck was it?" Remy asks, shocked by what she's hearing.

"I'm getting to that, girl, hang on," Raquel says.

"After sitting there for a bit, I decide to make a run for it. Mind you, I wanted to wait until dusk. Things are darker then, and it makes it difficult for the sniper to pick me off."

"Damn, that's smart!" Tonya says.

"I made the decision to draw his fire since I knew his location. I found a boot and a 38 Special with ammunition in the glove compartment of Kellie's Jeep after crawling to the back of it. Tossing the boot out, I was ready to fire, if necessary."

"Did he fire?" Remy asks with excitement.

"OMG, girl, will you chill out?" Raquel says. "I'm getting to that."

Remy giggles and rolls her eyes.

"I shot the boot out, but nothing happened. At all. You've no idea how disappointed I was, since I was ready to go to war."

The girls laugh and wait for her to continue.

"After that, I just stayed alert and waited for dusk. I . . ."

Raquel's eyes narrow. She senses that they're not alone anymore. She stands and makes her way to the door, looking out toward the beach. This, of course, draws both of the girls' attention and concern.

"What's wrong?" Remy asks.

Raquel's eyes sweep up and down the beach. Nothing seems amiss. She shrugs and then returns to her spot near the fireplace.

"It's nothing," she says.

Raquel tops up their wine glasses and settles back down. With one quick glance at the door, she continues her story.

"So what happened next?" Tonya asks.

"I headed for the gate, but I found it locked once I got there."

"Fuck! The motherfucker was waiting for you, wasn't he?" Tonya prods once more.

Raquel's eyes narrow as she stares at Tonya. "Am I telling this story, or are you?"

Tonya laughs and settles back down with anticipation. "Sorry."

"That's okay. I back up under the trees near the shack. That's when I discovered where the journal might have been. Mind you, I realized I'd have to run the gate. You've no idea how bad I felt about that at the time. Can you imagine having to inform Kellie that I fucked up her Jeep?"

"I bet," Remy says.

"I felt bad. She's been so amazing in a lot of ways, and now I had to tell her that I fucked up her Jeep."

"Did you end up having to ram that gate?" Tonya asks.

"Nope. Things didn't turn out the way I thought they would. After I crawled away from the shack with the journal in hand, I found myself facing the sniper." Tonya and Remy's eyes open wide. "He was standing directly between me and the gate. I was prepared to run through him, and confidently grabbed the 38 Special in my right hand, ready to slam the accelerator."

"He shot at you?" Remy inquires.

"Fuck no. Next thing I know, the sniper is taken out by a sniper bullet shot from a great distance.

"How do you know that, and by whom?" Remy asks.

"You hear the shot, and then you see the hit. That means it was fired from a great distance," she clarifies. "I can only surmise, at this point, but I think my guardian angel was there watching my back."

"Fucking A, right! He was there for me, too," Tonya replies.

Raquel and Remy simultaneously turn and stare at her.

"He wasn't there for you, Tonya," Remy says, shaking her head in disbelief.

"Honey, he was there for Jason. You were lucky, that's all," Raquel adds.

Tonya realizes that they're right, but she is still reaping the accolades of her fifteen minutes so she just brought it up. "Well, maybe so, but he could have fucked me up if he wanted to and he didn't."

The group starts laughing uncontrollably.

****

SEVERAL HOURS LATER, the girls are sitting quietly in front of the fire, contemplating the story that has been told. They can't believe how things have gone for Raquel. It wasn't that long ago that they were just party animals, enjoying their pathetic lives, and now this is happening. Tonya reminds Raquel of the first time they met in jail. How they coincidentally hooked up and covered each other's backs during their stay.

"I remember when you dragged that dyke bitch into that room and almost beat the shit of her," Tonya says.

Raquel smirks with pride. "She deserved it."

"That guard had a hard-on for you until that happened. I think you scared the shit out of him," she recalls.

Raquel recalls how Tonya was there when she sitting in the release room, wondering where or what she was going to do. Then there she was, waiting outside. She remembers spending time at Tonya's house until she got her bearings. She reaches over and wraps her arms around Tonya's neck, tears welling up in her eyes.

Remy breaks the moment. "What are you going to do with the journal?"

Raquel doesn't answer right away. Her eyes are drawn to the door once more. She hears the Irish Setter barking outside. This is a tell-tale sign that her assassin is near.

"I put it in a safe place and made copies of it," she says. "If anything were to happen to me, the contents of that journal will be made public, and I don't think they want that to happen."

"Who is *they*?" Remy asks.

"I don't know that yet, but until I do, the journal will remain secure and hidden. I think I'm going to cut the night short. I'm tired."

Remy's eyes narrow. She knows her well and suspects a hidden agenda, but agrees to call it a night. They carry their glasses to the kitchen and exchange hugs, saying their goodnights.

Raquel walks them to their car and watches as they drive away. She then walks around the side of the house onto the beach, looking for the assassin. He is nowhere in sight and the Irish Setter is gone. She shakes her head and writes it off to paranoia. She enters the house from the beach and finds the assassin standing inside. He is holding a silencer. She is unafraid and shuts the door behind her.

"I take it that this isn't a booty call," she says with heavy sarcasm.

The assassin smiles and hides the revolver from

sight. "I need you to give me the journal, Raquel," he states with authority.

She plays coy. "What journal might that be?"

He smiles, but it isn't one of amusement. "Don't do that with me."

Remaining calm and collected, Raquel says, "I don't know about any journal. I do want to thank you for rescuing me at the ranch." A muscle twitches a long his lower jaw, a sure sign that he's reacting to her statement. "I went there to retrieve something, yes, but it wasn't any book. Fuck me or kill me. Either way, I'm okay with it."

This guy is a professional. He's heard all sorts of begging and nervous explanations. The fact that she isn't fazed by him disturbs him. He's not sure if she's lying or not at this point. He flashes the silencer in her direction, hoping it'll cause a reaction. To his dismay, it does not.

"You are a very complex and cool customer, but I have to warn you now. I need the book, so if you have it, give it. And if you don't, then you don't."

Raquel doesn't flinch. She smiles at him. "I don't even know your name," she says.

He says nothing before he approaches her and lightly kisses her on the forehead. He then exits onto the beach.

14

A LONG, SLEEPLESS NIGHT follows Raquel's last night there. She wakes up early and sits on the beach with a cup of coffee, enjoying the sunrise, planning what to do next. She has almost committed the journal to memory, and believes it's time to confront the ones she knows are on the list.

Raquel decides that if they deny it, it won't matter. The journal will be delivered to the powers that be, and the results will be the same. She knows the reason as to why Billy is on the list. There's no need to bother him. He wouldn't deny it, anyway.

After calling Remy and Tonya to check in, Raquel heads for the Golden Cadillac in Canoga Park. She has called ahead, asking Rob to meet her there instead of his house. She feels that it's better to meet in a place where there isn't so much confusion and chaos.

✳✳✳✳

ABOUT AN HOUR LATER, Rob walks into the Golden Cadillac and looks for Raquel. He makes his way to the bar. Erin, the bartender, points to the back. Rob spots Raquel sitting in the booth on the right side near the back room. He slowly walks in her direction, and slides into the booth with a smile.

"Common ground?" he asks.

Raquel doesn't say anything at first. She stares at the man she thought she could trust. He's someone who took her in and gave her sanctuary when things were really bad. He waits for her to talk. After several minutes of contemplation, she breaks the silence.

"Am I not family to you?" she asks. "Did I not prove my worth and take a hit for this family?"

Rob knows what's coming and he explains before she gets too far into it. "You are family. That's why you are still alive. It's not me you want, Raquel. I'm just a guy on a list. A guy that has a business to run. A guy with lots of responsibility."

"You could have told me the truth!"

"No, I couldn't. It was nothing more than business. If you'd just stayed out of it . . ."

Raquel sighs. "You know, I met a great guy who has a hidden agenda. He's not the guy I thought he was at all. He's related to a Mexican Cartel leader who filters drugs and money into this country. The big joke on me is that I loved this guy and stood by him. Hell, I was married to his cousin, for Christ sake! The mystery book has a lot of names, dates, and numbers in it. It just so happens that you *might* be on that list.

What a fucking coincidence, huh?"

Rob stares at her straight in the face, and shows no signs of remorse or guilt. "This is a business, Raquel. I didn't betray you. I'm the one who told you where Miguel was hiding out. I'm on your side."

"Of course, you did. You wanted me to get to him, so you could get the book," she counters.

"I don't need the book. Give it to me, and it's all over," he states. "If you hold out, things will only get worse. You've my word that I won't be a party to it, but I won't be able to stop them. I owe you that much, at least."

Raquel knows that if she is going to end this, it has to be done her way. "I need a favor, maybe the last one. I think I deserve this much," she says. "Set a meeting up for me with Eric's uncle. I want a face to face."

Rob thinks about it for a moment. "Okay, but you already know what's going to happen. If that's what you want, you can have it."

"I do."

"I'll make the call," he says.

He stands and starts to leave before she stops him.

"Where's Miguel?" she asks.

Rob glances at her out of the corner of his eye. He doesn't offer her an answer and exits instead. Raquel doesn't really care at this point, but the question on her mind is, *where the hell is he?*

RAQUEL KNOWS that she can count on Rob to keep his word and arrange the meeting with Eric's uncle. She wonders where it will be, and whether it might be the last few days she spends on this earth. With that in mind, she changes her mind about Billy and decides to go see him.

She arrives at the Chateau Marmont Hotel only to find out that Billy has gone on tour and he won't be back for months. It saddens her to think that she may never see him again. She doesn't want to leave things as they are between them without closure. He'd done the unthinkable, but she just wants to say that she forgives him. That closure, unfortunately, may never happen just like the closure she needs with Eric probably won't either. The problem with Eric is that he's in Blythe. She won't have time to go back there before the meeting, so things will have to fall where they fall.

On the ride back to Malibu, Raquel thinks of all the people that are important to her and how she should touch base with them in case the meeting goes wrong. The heaviest on her mind is her kids. She has a chance to get them back now. Any more drama, she'll lose them forever. She knows she has to see them before the meeting, in case everything goes bad. It would kill her to never see their faces again. She needs to spend some time with them so they know they are loved. It depresses her to think that they may never see her again, and she will have passed on the genes of "abandonment" to them.

Raquel decides that she'll call both Remy and Tonya, and give them an update. She chooses not to see them again until it is over. *There's no need to make it a goodbye,* she thinks. The situation is difficult enough, and she needs to stay focused.

****

THAT NIGHT, Raquel sits on the beach, enjoying a glass of wine, expecting to hear the Irish Setter, but it never happens. The assassin has chosen to step away. She sits there, anticipating the phone call from Rob about the meeting. She has already called Remy and Tonya. Although they are unhappy with her decision, they understand and will wait to hear from her when she gets back. In the meantime, they will say a few novenas in her name. Remy promises to look after her kids if things go wrong. Tears are shared over the phone by the three best friends.

One last thought passes through her mind. If she returns from this dark meeting, she decides that she will make a fresh start. She will petition to get her kids back and move home to the Temecula area, away from LA, so that her kids can have somewhat of a normal life. She will also focus on her real estate business. No more beach houses for her.

She also surrenders to her past indiscretions and accepts them. She did what she did and it's over. It's time to move on, to be proactive. She and her kids deserve it. If things don't work out, and she becomes a statistic, then so be it.

With that thought in mind, Raquel's cell phone rings. She answers it and listens to the instructions.

"I'll be there. Thank you, Rob," she says as she hangs up.

Raquel hates the timing. The visit with the kids will have to wait.

15

SANTA MONICA AIRPORT at 5:00 AM is very quiet. Raquel is sitting in the back of a limousine that was provided for her. Silence envelopes her as she anticipates the day and what it will bring while waiting for the incoming GV to land. She watches as the private jet lands and taxis over to her car as it idles on the private tarmac. The door of the jet opens and the chauffeur gets out, opening the door for Raquel. She gets out and walks slowly toward the jet, expecting to get some sort of reception, but no one steps out.

Raquel climbs the steps and takes one last look behind her before she moves inside. The door is closed by the copilot. She takes a seat.

"May I get you something?" he politely asks.

"Nothing for the moment, thank you," she responds.

"Please help yourself. It's a long flight. There is food and drink for your pleasure."

"Thank you."

The copilot goes back to the cockpit and shuts

the door. If this was meant to be a time for reflection and intimidation, then it is working. Raquel didn't expect them to roll out the red carpet, but six or seven hours of flight time with no company is not much different than the small cell she occupied in the Twin Towers.

During the long flight, Raquel helps herself to a few glasses of wine to calm her nerves. She enjoys the small meal and treats they've provided for her. Perhaps, it was meant to be her "last supper."

****

AS THE GV JET nears the Isthmus of Panama, Raquel takes interest and stares out the window at what could be considered a wonder of the world–the famous locks of Panama. It's just after noon, and she's enjoying the aerial view as the GV comes off the Atlantic into the Isthmus at water level, moving at high speed while approaching Limon Bay and the Gatun' Locks at the Panama Canal. As the jet nears the bay, it rises up over the Locks, moving toward Gatun' Lake.

Raquel can see a huge freight liner in Chamber #3 of the Gatun' Locks. Line handlers have attached large steel cables to the powerful electric locomotives called, mules, for towing. The Locks are closed and the water is flooding the main culverts connected to 100 holes in the floor of the chamber. For anyone who has never seen this operation, it's spectacular.

The GV passes the Lock and flies out over the lake. There are several ships moving across the twenty-three mile lake under their own power toward the other side of the canal. Raquel is in awe of the view, but she hasn't lost sight of why she is there. If this is the last thing she sees on this planet, then she has viewed splendor.

****

MINUTES LATER, the GV flies past the ships on the lake, heading for Gamboa, passing the Gatun' Dam. The waterway gradually narrows until the river turns under the bridge of the Panama Railroad.

Raquel can see the Gamboa marine division with heavy cranes, dredges, tugs, and barges as they approach the Gatun' Chamber #3. She watches as the linemen release the cables, and the double set of locks are released as the mules come to a stop.

****

IT ISN'T LONG before the GV reaches the Miraflores Lake and the Pedro Miguel Locks. The pilot maneuvers the jet into its final approach to a private air field not far from the Pedro Miguel Locks.

"Mama, we are making our final approach, please be seated," the pilot announces over the intercom.

Raquel secures her belt for landing and watches as they make their approach, descending to the

205

private air field.

****

THE GV JET lands and taxis to a small hangar at the end of the runway, coming to a stop. A black Town car is waiting to take Raquel to her final destination. She has no idea where it is, nor has she been told who she is actually meeting, but she is expecting to see Eric's uncle.

Raquel maintains her calm demeanor and exits the GV, thanking the pilot as she walks to the Town car and gets in. The car pulls away. The ride to the plantation estate seems almost as long as the flight. She wonders if this was all planned. Just the same, she enjoys the ride with the mountains on her right and the Pacific Ocean on her left.

During this time, Raquel thinks about all the things she's accomplished throughout her young life, as well as all the hardship she's overcome. As she reflects on it all, she can honestly say she's risen above how she was raised. There have been times in her early life that she felt it would be a short life, but she stayed the course. With the help of close friends, she's survived and endured it all.

****

TWO HOURS have now gone by. The Town car approaches the security gates of a very large Panama estate. The chauffeur honks the horn of the car and the gates open. The car drives through and stops again. The gates close behind it.

Raquel can see that they are in a holding area, and there is another set of gates in front of them. To their right is a security building with high-tech equipment, including a satellite dish on top of the roof.

Two security guards approach the car and check it thoroughly. They have long poles with mirrors and detectors that sweep under the car. Once they establish that the car is clean, the second set of gates open and the car passes through. On the other side, a white GMC awaits them. Once in sight, it escorts the Town car up to the main house.

Raquel isn't surprised by the extent of the security. This whole issue isn't being driven by a small organization. This is drug cartel and money laundering territory.

She enjoys the long ride up to the main house. She can see several large bungalows along the way that sit on either side of an 18-hole golf course. On the right, there is a lake and several bungalows. This estate is surrounded by the mountains on the right, and she can see the Pacific Ocean on her left. The estate sits high, so the ocean is quite a distance away.

The GMC escorts them to the main entrance of this amazing home that is approximately 20,000 square feet. Raquel has noticed that security guards are positioned throughout the property the entire way up to the house. All of them are carrying semi-automatic weapons. This would be classified as a fortress more than an estate.

For the first time, Raquel feels that she might be in way over her head and wonders if it was worth it as the Town car comes to a stop. Of course, it's too late. She asked for this meeting and she got it. At this time, she is received by house staff and escorted inside. They look to see if she might have brought luggage, but Raquel wasn't treating this as a holiday. She came with nothing but the clothes on her back.

As she enters the huge house, she glances about the massive entrance. There is nothing but decadence and wealth in every direction, including priceless art. She's slowly escorted through the manor. Along the way, she catches glimpses of drugs as they are laid out like food. Half-naked and half-stoned women are lying around as though they own the place.

It's not unlike the night she attended the event at the gallery. People stare at her as she walks along. Some looks are inviting and sensual in nature. Some are blank, while others are threatening.

Raquel is escorted to a very large suite in the west wing of the manor. She is left on her own with no instructions. As the large doors to the suite are shut, she sits on the bed, staring around the room.

"What the fuck?" she says, speaking for the first time since her arrival.

****

HOURS PASS, and no one comes to Raquel's suite. In defiance, she sits in the exact same place, staring at the door while sitting in the darkness. She hasn't moved to go to the bathroom or shower. *If this is a test of tolerance,* she thinks, *then they're challenging the wrong person.* She sits and stares.

The door soon opens, and two Latin guards step inside carrying semi-automatics. Raquel stands and follows them out without saying a word. She follows them back to the main portion of the house, and is presented to a very large Latin man wearing an LA Laker's warm-up outfit. He is wearing sandals and is adorned from head to toe in bling and gold. Two girls stand on either side of him, half-naked, pleasing him whenever he suggests it. He is drinking a Mojito and shows no signs of stress in his life. As Raquel approaches, he spins around to face her with a huge smile on his face.

"Welcome to Panama," he says with a smile. "Sorry for the long delay. I hope you have been made comfortable."

Raquel doesn't change expression. She's seen this machismo bullshit before and it does not impress her. For some reason, Latins or blacks from other countries think they're more intimidating than the US born Latins or African-Americans.

That dog doesn't hunt, she thinks.

She smiles politely at him. "I'm fine, thank you."

He knows she hasn't moved for hours, and that tells him that he isn't dealing with the typical

209

American. From what he's been told, she can handle any situation without fear or intimidation, but he had to test it for himself. He makes a motion of his hand and a personal bodyguard immediately approaches her, pressing a silver-plated 9MM against her temple.

Raquel never budges or reacts. She stares straight ahead at him, not taking her eyes from his. The bodyguard cocks the hammer, and still, she does not move.

"Fucking balls, this woman has," he states, laughing out loud as if it's all a joke. He waves his hand about, and the bodyguard steps back.

"I didn't come here for games. And I would guess that you are the reception community," she confidently states.

The Latin's smile disappears, turning to a menacing stare. "You're fucking with the wrong people," he says with a very strong Latin accent.

"No, you are fucking with me," she replies. "And I'm holding aces."

The bodyguard moves toward her again and holds the 9MM against the side of her head. She never moves. The Latin waves him off once more.

"Let's do her now, like we've been told," he says, waving the 9MM around like he can't stand the wait. He so desperately wants to put a bullet in her brain.

"I make the decisions here, so back off," he commands.

The bodyguard steps back, but soon keeps moving forward, jabbing her with the 9MM to let her know that he wants her bad.

Raquel laughs a little, and it makes him mad. "Please don't say it. It's such a cliché!"

Of course, the bodyguard has no idea that she is referencing the *Dirty Harry* famous line. The large Latin smiles again, since he gets the reference, and offers her a drink.

"Mojito?"

"Why the fuck not?" Raquel replies.

One of the girls pours the Mojito and hands it to Raquel, staring at her with very wanting, seductive eyes.

"Miriam likes you. You can have her if you like."

Raquel smiles and accepts the Mojito. "Why don't we just cut to the chase? You, obviously, are not the man I came to see."

The smile on his face disappears, and now it's all business. He takes a few moments to gather himself. He shares a kiss or two with each girl and takes a drink. He then directs his focus to Raquel.

"It's like this. You are my guest for . . . let's say, the next couple days. Enjoy yourself with all the refreshments. We will see what we are to do with you then."

This is not what Raquel expected to happen at all. Now that she is behind this fortress, she is aware that there is no escaping. She is stuck and will have to make the best of it. The challenge comes in the guise of maintaining her sanity. More importantly, she knows she needs to stay clear of this particular bodyguard, who wants nothing more than to put a bullet in her face and bury her somewhere, perhaps in the Pacific Ocean.

"I wasn't expecting to be on holiday. Nor did I bring any luggage. Two or three days is a huge disappointment," she says.

He looks around before he answers. "I think you can find what you need here. Pick a girl. Their closets are full," he says.

Raquel expects as much, but she has to try anyway. "When can I expect to have my meeting, since that's the purpose of my coming here?"

The Latin smiles again and says, "Your purpose here is in our hands now. So accept my hospitality and enjoy yourself. I will let you know when news comes."

****

LATER THAT NIGHT, Raquel is invited to the dining room table to share a meal with the Latin and all of his entourage, including a host of beautiful women. The food and drink is expensive and everyone seems to be enjoying the moment. All except Raquel.

She maintains her calm exterior, but on the inside she is raging. She smiles and looks down the long table to the Latin, who she actually finds attractive. Under different circumstances, she would want to fuck him. She picks at her food and watches the show.

The Latin notices her quiet demeanor. "Don't care for the food? Perhaps, I can have something else prepared."

Raquel looks up and smiles. "No, it's wonderful. I was just thinking," she says.

"About what?"

"Life is a challenge, at best," she replies. "It's not necessarily about the goal line, but more about the journey itself."

He finds it odd that under these circumstances, Raquel is putting a spiritual spin on things. He never expected to hear something like that from her. Her appearance, and what he knows about her, is a direct opposite to her statement. He would like to know more, but doesn't inquire further.

"The fucking bitch is supposed to be dead, Julio," the bodyguard whispers. "That's what we were told, and it's your ass."

His words are heard along the entire length of the table. Everyone turns to looks at Raquel. She pretends that she hasn't heard what he's said.

"Something wrong?" she asks.

All eyes turn to Julio. He smiles.

"Please excuse me for one moment," he says as he gets up. He motions for the bodyguard to leave the table and follow him.

Raquel watches them walk out to the pool area and an argument ensues. The Latin is livid with the bodyguard. He pulls out a fancy revolver from under

213

his wardrobe, and he holds it directly to the man's forehead. The words cannot be heard, but everyone knows the context of his statement.

Things calm down. They return to the table and take their seats. The bodyguard sits submissively, but he stares down the table at Raquel and winks, sending her a silent message. He holds his hand to his temple and pretends to put a bullet in his head. It's his way of telling her that her time on this earth is about to end, and he will be the one to carry out the execution.

Raquel smiles, but inside, she is falling apart. She masks it with humor. "Did you get a spanking?" she asks the bodyguard.

The bodyguard jumps to his feet and rushes to her side, shoving his 9MM in her face. He cocks the hammer and desperately wants to pull the trigger. The entire table gets up and steps back in anticipation of the execution. The Latin sits calmly, eating his food, waiting for the bodyguard to do it. He slowly lifts his revolver and sets it on the table next to his plate. After a few threatening moments, he backs away, knowing that if he fires his gun, his life is over.

"Down boy!" Raquel jokes.

He may not be able to kill her, but he strikes her across the face, knocking her out.

****

TWO HOURS LATER, Raquel awakens. She is lying on her bed in complete darkness. She feels the side of her face. It is sore. She has been hit before, so no damage is done except for the headache. She would have liked nothing better than to have taken the punch and stared the bodyguard down in the face, but it didn't happen that way. He has one up on her, but she has to accept the fact that she provoked him and she's still alive.

Raquel sits up and looks around the dark room. She sees that someone has been in there, and has left a wardrobe for her in the master closet. She walks to the closet and finds a warm-up outfit, making the decision to get more comfortable. First, she'll take the long-awaited shower. She throws the outfit on the bed, and soon retires to the bathroom.

****

AN HOUR LATER, Raquel is dressed and making her way cautiously through the large manor toward the kitchen. She really didn't finish dinner, so she is feeling a tad peckish, as they say. She would like a cup of tea, or perhaps a glass of wine.

She reaches the kitchen area. To her surprise, she hasn't encountered anyone. No bodyguards are seen. There are a few nude girls in the large pool outside, but they aren't a bother to her. She makes her way into the kitchen and goes straight to the refrigerator. In it, she finds a nice combination of cheeses, meats, and vegetables, all perfect for a late night snack. Low and behold, she finds an open bottle of very expensive white wine. She prepares a nice plate and pours herself a glass of wine, sitting down at the table, intent on enjoying the snack.

A strong accented voice breaks the silence. "A night person, I take it," Julio says.

He enters and heads for the refrigerator to prepare a snack for himself. Raquel offers to share hers with him. He accepts and finds a glass, approaching the table. He sits and she pours him a glass of wine.

He takes a sip and then stares at her with confusion. "You know you made a mistake coming here. It was a set-up," he states.

Raquel doesn't say anything, at first. "That was a possibility, but as I said before, I am holding aces."

He smiles. "Well, maybe kings," he answers with humor. "Why did you take the chance in coming here? What do you hope to gain from it all? Everyone has a motive or hidden agenda. What's yours?"

"This might seem foolish to you, but I've endured a lot in life," she says. "I've surpassed more than nine lives, though I probably should have been dead long ago. From an early age, I've always believed that I was destined for something, not necessarily greatness, but something significant."

The Latin understands this, especially since he, too, has endured a great deal in his lifetime. "I respect your conviction, but it can get you killed."

"I'm not afraid to die. I've faced death before, so this is just another journey."

He realizes that she's made another spiritual reference, one he contemplates. "So you are not afraid to die?"

"No, I have no fear of death," she responds.

He smiles and thinks about that for a moment before he plays his next hand. "Maybe there is something greater that would detour you rather than your own death."

Raquel finds his question to be calculating and quite revealing. She knows he is about to deliver a bomb.

"And what might that be?"

The Latin stands and invites her to follow him. "Bring your glass with you."

Together, they pick up their wine glasses, and he brings along the bottle. They make their way to the pool area and surrounding gardens. They walk in silence as they pass by the pool and the party that's going on. Some of the nude women are enjoying the night, the water, and each other, toasting drinks and party favors of all kinds.

Once they are past the pool, they walk down a long path in the garden. Nothing but silence surrounds them. They approach several bungalows near the back of the garden. It's quiet. Raquel wonders if he's going to seduce her or deliver the last blow.

They approach a bungalow. A guard stands by the door. He opens the door and steps aside. The Latin and Raquel enter. It is very dark and quite difficult to see. The atmosphere resembles that of an opium den. Although the estate is elegant in nature, this room is a poor reflection of that. It is filthy and smelly.

Raquel looks across the room. Though she can barely see, there is a naked man lying face down on the bed. His right wrist is handcuffed to the bed. A very dark-skinned girl, obviously stoned out of her mind and also naked, is passed out next to him. It doesn't take long before Raquel recognizes Miguel. His face isn't visible, but she knows it's him. His body has been beaten and he's been allowed to get drunk or high until they decide what to do with him.

The Latin gauges Raquel's reaction, but there is none. He is surprised, if not shocked. Raquel has no love for her man, but seeing him this way is heart-wrenching. She can remember times like this when she was on a binge, seeking a train wreck life. She doesn't spend much more time viewing this dungeon and walks out without saying a word.

This further leaves the Latin feeling completely confused. Perhaps he was wrong about her, after all. He thought this might be a pressure point, something that would make her crack, but her lack of reaction tells him differently.

****

IT DOESN'T TAKE LONG for them to return to the house and the kitchen. Raquel sits back down to finish her snack and remains silent. The Latin has played his hand, and now he has to know why.

"He is your man, right?" he inquires.

"He *was* my man," she reveals.

The Latin rolls his eyes and now understands the disconnected feeling between them. "So no love lost, I see."

"Nope."

"Carlos arrives the day after tomorrow," he says. "You will have your meeting, and then a decision will be made." He stands and moves toward the pool area.

Raquel doesn't turn around. "Why is Miguel here?"

He turns to face her once more. "He is accountable to the family," he states, leaving Raquel alone to enjoy the rest of her snack and evening.

Raquel sits there for a moment before she decides to retire to her room. She picks up the snack plate and opens the refrigerator to retrieve another bottle of wine. She then heads for her room.

Moments later, she arrives at her door, sensing the presence of someone nearby. She pushes the door open. Lying on the bed is a very exotic and beautiful young Latin stud. There is not one ounce of fat on his body.

Raquel hesitates for but a moment. She then steps inside and shuts the door behind her. An Adonis gift has been presented to her. She obliges, since tomorrow may be a day of reckoning.

AFTER ABOUT AN HOUR of nuru heaven, Raquel is lying face down on the bed, and the very muscular dark-skinned Adonis is using his powerful hands and body to sooth her body with oils. For an entire hour, she has forgotten all about her problems and has fallen into ecstasy. As she enjoys his powerful touch, his inner sensual demons begin to rise again. He mounts her from behind. She cries out as he penetrates her, lifting her ass up toward him in an arched move.

Just outside the large glass door on the veranda, the Latin stands with his back to the wall, listening as Raquel is driven toward nuru heaven once more. He smiles and walks away. Raquel glances at the veranda, knowing the entire time that he was hidden as a voyeur.

She smiles.

16

FOURTY-EIGHT HOURS PASS and not much changes in that time. Raquel accepts the hospitality of the Latin. She spends most of her time alone, but from time to time, she'll seek him out to have small talk. He learns a great deal about her during their talks, and has begun to like her. Unfortunately for her, he never makes a move toward her in a sexual way. She hopes he would, but he never does. During one of their intense talks, Raquel feels comfortable enough to talk about her kids, and how things went bad for her.

"I've accepted total responsibility for my actions. It's my dream to have my kids returned to me. I believe it'll happen soon," she says. "*If* you don't take me on a ride to the Pacific."

The Latin doesn't say much about his life, but she can tell that he must have had a childhood similar to hers. He doesn't say where he's from, but she surmises that it's Panama. He has a way about him, a charm. She believes he is from money and has chosen

221

to journey to the dark side just as she has done. Their talks are brief, but filled with contentment and understanding.

During the night, Uncle Carlos arrives with his entourage. Raquel waits for her audience with him. He is sealed away in the east wing, and she is kept separate from him. She ventures out of her room, but it's only when she's allowed to do so.

Today, the bodyguards are everywhere. Everyone is on alert, and there is more tension in the air than usual. Raquel recalls meeting Uncle Carlos in LA. She will never forget that night or that dinner. Eric's aunt was a bitch to her, and she hopes she won't be here, If she is, she'll just deal with it.

Raquel is asked to stay in her room until she's called. She remembers that Carlos isn't that intimidating, although Eric was always nervous around him. Now she knows why. She has decided that she'll treat him the same way she treats Rob. Both men have the power to end your life, but if you just act like it doesn't matter, perhaps things will turn in your favor.

She decides that no matter what, her main objective is to offer them a fair deal. She will give them what they want, and in turn, they will give her what she wants. Deep down, she believes that this is possible, or she wouldn't have come.

Memories of her private time with the assassin surface. He always told her that the key to any situation like this is to make them feel that you are doing them a favor. That it is all in their hands, and you are just providing a service. She also remembers that he used the words "passive-aggressive" a lot. While she waits in her room, she wonders if the assassin will be there. The thought brings a smile to her face.

****

IT ISN'T LONG BEFORE they send a bodyguard for Raquel. She is taken to the closed dining room area. She waits outside the door for several moments while Uncle Carlos finishes an earlier meeting. He must have risen early because it is only 7:30 AM, and he is on his third meeting. Finally, the door opens and she enters the cigar smoke filled dining room.

Seated at the other end of the dining table is Uncle Carlos. To Raquel's disappointment, Eric's aunt sits to the right of him. To his left is the Latin, and opening the door was the aggressive bodyguard that waits for the moment he can put a bullet in her brain. He believes in his heart that today is that day.

Raquel is shown to a seat to the left of the Latin, and she takes it with a smile. A lovely breakfast is laid out, and a plate is placed in front of her.

"Breakfast is served," the uncle says.

For about an hour, nothing is said. Everyone eats in silence. The uncle never takes the fork from his mouth or looks up. He enjoys his food, and no one dares to interrupt him, including the aunt. Raquel remembers that from the first time they met. The aunt has unsolicited opinions, but only at the appropriate times. Once the uncle finishes his meal, he looks toward Raquel.

"Excellent breakfast, wouldn't you say, Raquel?" he asks.

"Indeed," she answers.

She remembers to be passive-aggressive and to always narrow your answers. It prevents chatter and arguments.

Uncle Carlos studies her for a moment, and then gets down to business. "You have something that belongs to me. Something that Miguel took from me by mistake. Very stupid boy, my Miguel."

Raquel doesn't answer right away. She turns her attention to the aunt. Keeping her face impassive, she delivers her answer in a slow, yet direct manner.

"With all due respect, I won't do business with you with her in the room."

The aunt is immediately offended and calls her out. "You fucking tramp, you don't dismiss me from the room. Ever!" she screams.

Raquel turns her focus back to the uncle and waits for his response. He looks at her and then at the Latin, before his eyes settle on Raquel once more.

"Okay," he says with authority.

The aunt is livid, but she knows better than to challenge him in front of everyone. She almost refuses to get up, but the bodyguard pulls her seat back and she is escorted from the room.

Raquel takes great satisfaction in this. She has turned the tables, only this time, she did not whisper in a restaurant. She spoke openly and directly so she could hear it. Once the door closes behind her, Raquel turns her focus back to the uncle.

"You can have your journal with conditions," she states.

Uncle Carlos is not accustomed to being dictated to. He doesn't find her amusing. He holds up his hand to stop her offer. He glances at the Latin before his eyes rove about the room, trying to calm the anger that is building within him. Eric is family and she married into that family, but business is business.

He breaks his silence and says, "Eric was given a responsibility to this family. He did well and stayed in line, but his worthless cousin, Miguel, is a different story. He continuously disrespected my family. His behavior was overlooked several times, but it has to stop. I used my influences to help him, but he shit on it every time. Yes, he is a good boy, but he is also a fuck up."

He hesitates for a moment, and then continues his speech. "He gets busted for nonsense, and I get him released. When he is released, he goes back to his old ways. He thinks he can disrespect me."

His anger starts to build inside once again. Uncle Carlos is not accustomed to having to explain himself to someone else.

"I don't even know why I bother telling you this sad story," he continues. "Miguel decided to split away from the family and take insurance. My fucking nephew breaks into the bank with a baseball cap and sunglasses on, and attempts to rob the fucking bank. He doesn't take cash, but he does force the bank manager to open my safe, taking only my journal!"

Raquel now knows how it all began. She smiles, which does not please Uncle Carlos at all.

"You find this fucking amusing, girl?" he asks in anger.

"No, Uncle Carlos," she says. "I find it pathetic."

Raquel has called him Uncle Carlos for the first time, and that shows respect. He listens as she tells him about the events of that day and many other days just like it. That she married Eric because he was a good man. Despite things going bad between them, she stood by him, but it didn't matter. He went away and her life went to shit. He meant everything to her and the kids. He had been a good husband and father to her kids, but now he is gone and that is that. Then, there is Miguel.

"No need to talk to you about Miguel. You already know about that," she states. He nods. "Yes, Uncle Carlos, Miguel is a fuck up."

Again, she uses his name with respect, and his inner anger begins to subside. He listens as she finishes her tale. She reminds him about her time with Eric, and how it all went down with him. He robbed a silly bank down the road and all hell broke loose. They traced Eric back to their house, and the Feds, local police, and just about every law enforcement agency arrived at her door. Her kids were frightened to death and crying, and she was treated like dirt. Of course, Eric was taken away and she was left to deal with the collateral damage.

"So, yes, Uncle Carlos, I've endured a lot for this family. Now, about your journal. I'll gladly give it back to you, but I ask for your forgiveness, and only wish to have a condition that protects me and mine," she pleads.

Uncle Carlos considers her words. "What is it that you want in exchange for the journal?"

Raquel looks him straight in the face, and calmly lays out her conditions. "I'll leave LA altogether and return to the Murrieta area where I grew up. I'll take my kids and not look back. Most of all, I want to build my real estate business. That's my focus and pledge. I've been left an inheritance from my maternal grandmother, and I plan to use that to get things started. I only ask that you use your influence with the mystery man to help me get my kids back. Then I'll disappear for good."

He regards her through veiled eyes, waiting for her to finish.

"Oh, and one last thing," she says. "For insurance and protection, I will keep the journal in a safe place, in case something were to happen to you. Your death would break our agreement, and that leaves me vulnerable."

Uncle Carlos begins to warm up to her. He realizes what an asset she could be to him.

"Are you sure you don't want to become a part of the family business?" he asks.

"No thanks, Uncle Carlos. I will choose the simple life from now on. I owe it to my kids," she states.

He laughs and understands the obligations of family. He looks at her hard and wonders if he should agree such a thing.

"I could just have you disappear altogether, and go in search of this journal myself," he says. "In time, I'm sure I'll figure out its location."

Raquel knows that this might be true, but it is also a risk, because he has no idea as to what she did with the journal and who might be standing in the wings if Raquel disappears. It could be someone with greater expectations, and that would make his life not so comfortable.

"You could do that, but it would be a risk, I think," she says with a smile.

Uncle Carlos understands her underlying meaning and smiles. She is threatening him, yet doing so in a passive-aggressive manner. He admires her approach and bursts into laughter. Everyone in the room joins in.

"Okay, ex-wife of my nephew," he says. "I will check with my partners and we will take your thoughts into consideration."

At this point, Raquel knows that Uncle Carlos is not the main man. He refers to partners, but no kingpin in a Cartel has partners. There is always just one and the other so-called partners are soldiers under the General. She was not expecting this. Now she will have to wait to see what fate brings to her doorstep. Although disappointed at this moment, Raquel still believes that a deal will be made. The journal must be returned, since it protects their network. She knows her conditions can be met with ease. They are non-threatening and modest. She didn't make large demands, so in her mind, it should be a deal they can make.

"When can I expect to get your answer?" she asks politely.

Uncle Carlos has not returned to his former self, and shows no signs of answering that question or any other question she might propose. He looks at the Latin, who, in turn, tells Raquel that the meeting is over.

She gets up and walks out of the room. As the door closes behind her, she can hear Uncle Carlos cursing in Spanish. His wrath has been released. This tells her that she is holding the aces once again, and she will just have to wait. She smiles and walks away.

****

THE NEXT MORNING, Raquel is sitting outside near the pool, enjoying her morning breakfast and coffee. Things have returned back to normal. Sometime in the late evening, Uncle Carlos and his entire entourage disappeared. Raquel discovered this fact when she left her room, and found that the dining room doors were left wide open. No more meetings were in progress. The birds had flown the coop.

What hasn't changed is the fact that the gun-toting bodyguard is still anxious and pacing around, wanting nothing more than to get the word that her offer has been denied so that he can have his way with her. Raquel constantly catches a glimpse of him in the shadows, staring at her. It makes her think of her guardian angel, the assassin. She admits to herself that she misses him.

Perhaps, one day we will meet again, she thinks.

As she continues to enjoy her breakfast, she catches a glimpse of the Latin coming from the back of the bungalow where they are keeping Miguel. She wonders if something has happened. She's made no stipulation in her deal for him. Perhaps, they have found him to be of no more use and have dispensed with him.

The Latin comes her way, but his approach is interrupted about halfway. The raging bodyguard is vehemently arguing with him about something. Raquel believes it to be about her. She watches as the Latin puts the bodyguard in his place, and then makes his way over to her.

"Good morning," he says as he sits down.

"Good morning, I think," she replies. "Trouble?"

"Not at all, just business."

"Me? Business?"

The Latin laughs and shrugs it off. "It's not always about you, Raquel," he says with a grin.

This is the first time the Latin has said her name. She wonders if this might be the appropriate time to mention Miguel. She decides to go for it, since he is in a good mood.

"Is Miguel in big trouble?" she asks.

The Latin's mood is not broken. He remains light and cooperative, and answers her inquiry with a smile. "He's in some trouble, but he will be forgiven, perhaps. No need to worry about him."

Raquel is happy to hear those words. Though no love is lost for Miguel, knowing that he is alive makes her feel better. She can go about her own business without having to explain his demise to the family.

"So . . . back to our midnight therapy sessions and glasses of wine," the Latin jokes.

Raquel smiles. "Yes, I enjoy our talks," she says.

The Latin turns serious and excuses himself. "So, until later," he replies as he walks away.

Raquel watches him disappear and wonders what a life with him would be like. She also wonders why she is always attracted to dark men with bad boy complexes. She decides that she will figure that all out later. Right now, she needs to get back home.

****

LATER THAT NIGHT, at approximately 2:00 AM, Raquel is awakened from sleep. She hears a huge argument taking place outside her door. For the first time in days, she is fearful of what might be happening. She sits up and stares at the door, waiting for hell to break loose. Moments later, the arguing stops. The Latin slowly opens the door and steps inside.

"Get dressed. You're going home," he states.

"Did you just get news?" she asks.

"Just do as I say, and get dressed," he says, and promptly walks out of the room.

Raquel jumps off the bed and rushes around the room to get dressed as instructed. She recognizes a sense of urgency in his voice, and the arguing outside the door tells her that the Latin is doing this on his own initiative. He hasn't heard back from Uncle Carlos.

Raquel slips on her clothes and exits the room in a hurry, taking only her personal items. Just outside the front door of the house, a heavily guarded black GMC is waiting. The Latin ushers her into the backseat. He is about to get in himself when the bodyguard, wielding his 9MM, rushes to the car. He is shouting in Spanish and waving his 9MM around like a crazy man who's possessed.

The Latin steps in front of him so that he has no access to Raquel as she sits in the backseat. Their argument escalates and threats are being thrown back and forth. Raquel understands Spanish quite a bit, so she knows about the threats being made. The bodyguard is telling the Latin that it will be his ass when Carlos hears about his decision. The Latin reminds his lieutenant that he is in charge here in Panama, and he will stand on his reputation and authority. He needs no authorization and the bodyguard needs to step back.

The bodyguard continues with his tirade as he paces back and forth, waving the 9MM in every direction at anyone that gets near him. He dances around the GMC, looking in through the dark smoked windows, trying to find Raquel. Finally, the Latin has had enough. He draws his weapon. Doing so provokes the other bodyguards into doing the same. All weapons are now pointing at the bodyguard. He is outmatched and he knows it.

"Fucking puta!" he says, and walks away.

The Latin gets in, and the GMC pulls away in a hurry.

****

TWO HOURS LATER, the GMC is sitting on the tarmac, and Raquel is escorted to the GV. The Latin gives instructions to the pilot to take her back to the Santa Monica airport with no stops in between. He takes Raquel's hand and kisses it. She squeezes it tight and kisses him on the lips.

"I will never forget you, Julio," she says.

Raquel boards the plane. The door closes, and the GV taxis away. The Latin watches the plane as it moves out onto the runaway, making its ascent into the dark sky. He smiles.

Raquel knows that he has taken a risk for her, and she will never forget it. It will be a long ride, but she is going home and that's all that matters. As she sits in the low light of the aircraft, she reflects on all that has happened, and tears begin to well in her eyes. Once again, vulnerability has reared its head.

17

THE SANTA MONICA SUNRISE is beautiful this special morning, not only for the residents of LA, but also for Raquel as the GV lands and taxis to the small terminal. A black Town car is waiting for her.

Raquel gets out and thanks the pilot for the safe ride home. She then gets in the Town car, and it pulls away. The Town car travels along the Pacific Coast Highway with the Pacific Ocean looming in the distance. Its destination . . . Malibu.

Raquel is sitting quietly, looking out through the smoky glass windows, staring at the serene setting. Her departure from Panama was so sudden that she was unable to notify her friends that she is on her way home. She decides that she'll call them once she gets to the beach house. There is a lot to talk about. Doing so over the phone is not an option.

She contemplates her next move. Uncle Carlos will most certainly have contacted the mystery man by now, and things will have been set into motion. She will gladly await that call. In no uncertain terms will she let this man know that she is now holding the cards. His bullshit will not be tolerated. She will get her kids back, and he better cooperate. No exceptions!

Raquel reflects on the last few days. For some unknown reason, she cannot shake the image of Miguel in that bungalow. She knows that he is a shit and deserves to pay, but she still has strong feelings for him. She would hate to see any harm done to him. How can she have so much anger for him and still wonder about his welfare? She keeps reminding herself that someday she will have closure there.

****

RAQUEL TAKES her time before calling her friends. She takes a shower and relaxes quite a bit, giving herself time to absorb all that has happened. There is no better place to do that than at the beach outside her door where she can feel the wind and mist coming in from the Pacific Ocean. She digs her feet into the sand and takes a sip from her wine glass. Happy hour has started early today.

Remy and Tonya will be over the moon with questions when she calls them. She will have to tell them that she has been home for most of the day. They will have hurt feelings, but she can endure that guilt. She needs this time to think about things. There are several things she has to do before she leaves town. Some will be personal and give her closure.

Others are just business.

She will have to sort out her issues with the county and her probation officer, and that's where the mystery man comes in. He is definitely on her priority list, but not at the top. It will be the last thing she does. As she sits enjoying the view, she glances down the beach and wonders about the assassin. She also wonders about the Irish Setter. It's enough to make her go exploring. She'll take a walk down the beach to the house where they first had their encounter. The worst that could happen is that she sees her friend, the dog, and she can say her goodbyes.

As Raquel reaches the beach wall and climbs the small stairs to the back yard, she finds the assassin sitting nearby, enjoying a glass of wine and petting the Irish Setter. The dog jumps up and rushes at Raquel with affection. She is completely shocked. All this time, she thought that he'd broken into the house and that the dog wasn't his, when, in actual fact, he lived there and he is the dog's owner.

"You crafty bastard!" she jokes.

He smiles and welcomes her with a kiss. "I see you made it back safe and sound."

Raquel is happy to see him, but wants to know why he didn't tell her that he lived there. It wouldn't have made a difference to her at all. She would have loved to know that he was available rather than waiting for him to come out of the shadows.

He invites her to sit down. He sees that her wine glass is empty and offers to pour her a glass. She accepts. He stares at her for a moment and smiles.

"I guess I won't be seeing you officially anymore," he states.

"I'm moving for sure. We will have to find another reason to get together," she answers. "Why you didn't tell me you lived here?"

"You already know the answer."

It sort of hurts her feelings, but she understands and lets it go. "Do I have a future with you in any way?" she asks.

"You already know that answer, too," he says once more.

"That hurts my fucking feelings," she says, sounding sad. "You could at least lie, like most guys do. I don't take abandonment well. And what the hell is your name?"

He laughs. "You are moving on and that's wonderful. Let's just leave it at that, for the time being."

Raquel likes the sound of that. She also recognizes that he has her details already, so he is aware of her plans and where she is going.

"I have a couple things to do before I leave, but I would like to spend some quality time with you."

He nods. "Quality time is good," he says.

"I'm meeting with Remy and Tonya, but I'm around later if you want to visit," she adds.

He nods once more. She stands and walks toward the sea wall. Raquel turns and looks back to find that he has gone inside already. Her smiles changes to a sad frown. She knows she will probably never see him again.

****

BY THE TIME she arrives back at the beach house, Remy and Tonya are there, sitting outside on the beach, waiting for her. When they spot her coming down the beach, they start to run and the reception is overwhelming. It's as though she has been away to war and has just returned. All three of them end up rolling around on the sand.

"What the fuck, girlfriend? Where have you been?" Tonya asks.

"She couldn't wait to get laid. That's where she's been," Remy says.

Raquel laughs at their disgusting humor. "I've been in the fucking trenches, thank you," she replies.

They stand and dust themselves off, walking back to the house. Once they are inside, Raquel brings out bottles of wine, and they get ready to settle in for what will be hour after hour of detailing the trip to Panama.

"Don't leave anything out!" Tonya says. "I want to hear everything down to the very last blow job."

They begin to laugh. Raquel is happy to see that Tonya has recovered from her time in Temecula.

****

FOR THE NEXT FOUR HOURS, Raquel documents her days prior to the trip and how she even got to Panama. The girls listen to every word she has to say.

"I went to see Rob. He owned up to his involvement in the situation, and made it possible for me to the meet with Uncle Carlos."

"So Uncle-fucking-Carlos is the kingpin?" Tonya asks.

"No, chill out, and let me tell the fucking story!" Raquel says. "I was picked up at the Santa Monica airport, not really knowing where I'm going, or if I'd come back. For six hours, I sat alone in the GV, graciously accepting the hospitality provided on the plane until I arrived in Panama City. Fuck, I flew in over the Locks, and that is one fucking sight to see!"

"What happened after that?" Tonya wonders.

"I was picked up and then spent another two hours in a Town car that took me to a very exclusive estate surrounded by a massive wall. It's heavily guarded and probably one of the most magnificent estates I've ever seen. I was treated with decadence, and there were pleasures in all shapes and forms."

"What the hell does that mean?" Remy asks.

"It means I was fucked, sucked, and fed well," Raquel quips. "My last supper, if you will."

The tone in the room changes immediately. Raquel laughs.

"Chill out, I'm here, aren't I?" she states. "Duh!"

Raquel goes on to tell them how the day by day

happened, and how the bodyguard wanted her ass bad. He would follow her around and hide in the shadows, at times, waiting to put a bullet in her head. She describes how the gorgeous Latin looked after her, and even pimped her out to an Adonis that rocked her world.

"Fucking hell, you get abducted, and you still get laid!" Remy says. "I don't believe you."

Raquel laughs. "I would have rather been fucked by the Latin, but the Adonis was awesome. The Latin would stand outside my suite and watch us fuck. It made me crazy hot, and I kept hoping he'd join us, but he never did."

Raquel's mood changes and she grows serious. "I saw Miguel. He was being kept in a bungalow, stoned and fucked up. I hate to admit it, but I honestly felt sorry for him."

"He deserved it, R," Tonya says.

"Yeah, maybe so, but it was difficult to see him like that," she replies.

"What happened to him?" Remy asks.

"I don't know. The Latin said that he would be okay, and I'm good with that. He'll just have to ride it out, just like Eric," she adds.

Remy and Tonya are astounded by the news. They want to know about Eric.

"I need closure with him. I can go on now, but he'll probably never see the light of day. I think I'll go see him one last time and tell him about Miguel."

"So, what about the journal?" Remy asks.

"I'll keep it for insurance," Raquel says. "I made a copy. I plan to give the copy to the mystery man before I leave town."

"What? Leave town!?" Remy and Tonya scream in unison.

Raquel knew this was coming. She didn't have the opportunity to tell her closest friends that LA is behind her. That she's moving back to Murrieta.

"It's time to move on, I think. I need to change my life and ways. Besides, it's not that far. We can still see each other," she says.

The entire room grows silent. Tears begin to well in their eyes. They understand completely, but she is their rock and entertainment.

"How the fuck are we going to party without you?" Remy asks.

Raquel is sad about the fact that she has to put this on them now, but it is time and they might as well get used to it. It will be only a few more days, and then she will be gone.

"There are things happening at the Fed building that will help me get my kids back. When that happens, I'm gone," she says.

Remy and Tonya hug her close. They are happy for her and remind her that they will always be there for her, no matter what.

The girls enjoy the rest of the night and fall asleep after finishing off the entire stock of wine. Raquel waits for the assassin to show, but he never does. Perhaps he doesn't want to come inside.

JUSTIFIABLY WOUNDED

Raquel invites her friends to sleep over. She knew that when she left his house, it was the last time she would see him. With all that has happened to her in the last month, she falls asleep without any difficulty, and sleeps the night through.

18

THE VERY NEXT MORNING, Raquel sets out for the valley to see Rob one more time. She would have stopped to spend time with Billy on the way, but he is still on tour, so she texts him instead and tells him of her plans. He answers back right away and says that he is happy for her. That he will always be a friend with benefits, and hopes she will stay in touch. Raquel texts him back and promises to stay in touch. She laughs and texts that she especially wants him to update her about his nasty exploits so she can get off thinking about it. He sends a 'LMAO,' and says he will.

Raquel calls ahead and asks that Rob meet her at the Golden Cadillac instead of the house. It's not that she didn't trust him, but it is in her best interest to try and put the old life behind her now. She travels the familiar roads to Canoga Park, reminiscing about the old days, laughing and crying a bit inside. They are behind her now, good or bad.

Raquel pulls into the Golden Cadillac parking lot.

Rob's Harley is parked outside. She enters the bar carrying a large envelope, and spots Rob standing at the bar, talking to the barkeep. She waves and approaches, receiving the normal hug and greeting from him.

"My girl, she's back and upright!" he jokes.

Raquel laughs. "Do you want to go to our booth in the back?"

"Sure."

They make their way to the back and sit down.

"Want anything to eat or drink?" he asks.

"No, thanks."

"So, it went well, I hear. You got what you wanted. That's good," he says.

Raquel slides the large envelope over to him to seal the deal. "Here it is, as promised," she states, taking a deep breath.

Rob doesn't even look inside. He looks at her with smiling eyes, and begins to ask about her plans. Raquel talks a little about the experience in Panama, but Rob doesn't seem interested. She cuts it short, and dives into her current plans.

"I'm getting my kids back. We made a deal. I meet them today, and hopefully, my ex won't make a fuss about it," she says.

Rob doesn't comment. He listens with an open heart, and hopes that she will make whatever decision is right for her.

"You do what is best for your family," he says. "It's always the best way."

Raquel and Rob spend the next hour or so talking about old times, and how much she appreciates his mentoring and advice over the years. She considers him family and a good friend. She's sorry about how things turned out, but there is always a reason for everything. Deep inside, she believes that moving away will do her some good.

Rob smiles and lays out one of his one-liners. "Who is Raquel?" he asks.

Raquel laughs and says she will use that from now on. That will become her mantra for the rest of her life. At this point, Rob seems a tad restless. She recognizes the signs and begs off to let him off the hook.

"Hey, I've got to go. Lots to do," she says.

He stands and picks up the envelope. Their gazes clash and her eyes well up.

"Don't be a stranger!" he replies.

They walk out together. Rob gives Raquel his normal bear hug. He mounts his Harley and rides away. He screams over his shoulder as he disappears.

"Who is Raquel!?"

Raquel looks up and down the street, and smiles in his direction for a second before she dries her tears. She drives away with no regrets. She's kept her word and delivered the copy of the journal as promised. The deal has been sealed.

****

ON HER WAY BACK to Malibu, Raquel decides to briefly visit all the places around the valley that meant anything to her. She drives by old apartments and buildings, and the places where she worked. It is a way of getting closure, something she's always wanted to do. Unfortunately, that's not always possible.

Tomorrow will be a big day for her. The kids are being dropped off for the weekend, for the first time in a very long time. She hopes that it'll go well. Her ex, in principle, has agreed to primary custody. With the endorsement of the system, Raquel's long time wish is coming through. The system is finally doing something for her, even though she blackmailed him into it.

Raquel has been in touch with the mystery man and a meeting has been arranged. She definitely wants closure there, so she's asked him to meet her before she leaves town. It isn't to his liking or wish, but he has been told that he should accommodate her. She has kept her side of the bargain, so he should be cordial and keep the peace.

*****

IT'S BEEN A COUPLE WEEKS since Raquel has been back to her own home. Now that the heat has been turned down, she decides it's time to go home . . . her home. Tomorrow is the first day of the rest of her life, and she wants to be ready for the kids. Her ex has agreed to bring them for the weekend.

Raquel pulls up to the house. It looks exactly as she left it. She thinks that although it's only been a few weeks, it seems like a lifetime. It's small, but it's hers, and she will make it comfortable for the kids. If all goes as planned, she will be on her way south soon enough.

Raquel steps inside and looks around. Everything is as she left it. It almost feels like a hotel room to her now. She makes her way to the refrigerator, and discovers a bottle of white wine. She pops the cork and settles down for a moment. She reminisces about the time she spent with Eric before he was arrested. How she'd met him and they instantly fell in love. He was good for her, she admits, and she was definitely good for him, but it's gone now. She wonders if she will love again, or if it'll be elusive for the rest of her life. Her thoughts are interrupted by the sound of the phone ringing.

"Hey, yeah, I got back forty-five minutes ago. Just checking things out for tomorrow," she says, briefly filling Remy in.

Remy suggests that she bring the kids to the beach house. They'd love it.

"They might love it, but asshole and his bitch won't. I'll get nothing but grief. No way," she counters. "Besides, I'll see them again shortly."

She hangs up. Finishing her glass of wine, she pauses the past. Perhaps one day, she can write about it, and make sense of the journey she has chosen.

"Hell, Winston Churchill was right. If you are

going through shit, don't stop. Or something like that," she says with a laugh.

Raquel looks around and then heads for the beach. Her list is getting short. She doesn't have much left to do, aside from collecting her kids, saying goodbye to Remy, Tonya, and a few others, and then getting the hell out of Dodge. Well, that's after she has her showdown with the mystery man. It might be a few more weeks, maybe a month, but she knows that she is done with Los Angeles.

19

LATER THAT NIGHT, Raquel meets with her two best friends. Tomorrow, the kids are being dropped off, and she'll have them for the weekend. That's the plan, at least. Her ex is a drunk, so anything could happen. Hell, she might even get lucky, and he'll just leave them with her for good.

The three amigos are sitting in their favorite spots on the beach, sharing a bottle of wine and shots of Tequila. The mood is pretty much the same as it was the last time they met. All three anticipate the passage of time before they meet up again.

"We know you won't be back up here, so we'll come to you for awhile," Remy vows.

Raquel reminds them that she isn't gone yet. She still has to give ample notice at work and finalize things with the hubby. She follows that up with a confession.

"I need some time away. You can all visit later on," she says.

She continues with an explanation about her

business partners being in LA. Because of this, she can't stay away forever. While they sit and think about it, Raquel glances around the beach, hoping to see the Irish Setter. She soon gets a brilliant idea.

"Hey, you guys want to meet my assassin and his dog?" she asks, trying to brighten things up.

Remy and Tonya immediately warm up to the idea.

"Fucking A, right," Tonya says.

The three walk across the beach toward the assassin's house. Raquel secretly hopes that he is there, but knows that's a long shot. As they get to the sea wall, she climbs the stairs and looks around. There is no sign of him or the dog, and there are no lights on in the house.

"Bust! He's not here," she says with disappointment.

Remy and Tonya share the same sentiment, though they are happy that she's willing to share him, if even for a moment.

"Oh, well," Remy says. "It's his loss. He could have had us all in one magnificent night!"

They laugh and move back down the sand, heading for the beach house.

"Raquel, this really sucks," Tonya says.

"I know."

They continue to walk. Within seconds, they break into a run, diving in and out of the surf.

****

ABOUT AN HOUR LATER, they are finishing up a bottle of wine as Raquel's cell phone rings. She answers it, feeling a slight trepidation.

"Hello?" She listens to the familiar voice. Her mood is no longer somber. "You have the right address, right?"

"Yes," her ex says.

"I'll be there bright and early." She hangs up. "Dickhead is dropping the kids off in the morning."

The phone rings again and she answers. "What, you forgot already?" she asks.

Her face goes blank. It's time to meet the mystery man. She is given instructions for the meeting place. She listens and acknowledges that she knows the place, and will be there within the hour. She hangs up.

"Was that him?" Remy asks.

Raquel nods and gets up. "You guys wait for me. I won't be long," she says.

She hurries inside and is out the front door in a flash. She wants this over with so that she can be free and clear on all accounts. Most of all, she wants closure.

****

RAQUEL MAKES her way down the Pacific Coast Highway to Alice's restaurant, the designated meeting place. She wants it to take place in public, in case the mystery man becomes difficult. He's chosen Alice's on Malibu Pier. After a short drive, Raquel arrives at Alice's and heads inside. She makes her way to the bar and looks around, but she sees no sign of the mystery man or his secret service entourage. She figures he will probably wait in the limousine and send an agent in to retrieve her, so she orders a drink and waits.

Forty minutes go by, and Raquel starts to get angry. She has been jerked around, and it pisses her off. She decides that she will wait ten more minutes, and then she is out of there. Those ten minutes pass, and there is still no sign of the mystery man. She finishes her drink, throws her payment down on the counter, and exits the restaurant.

As she reaches the parking lot, she looks around. There's no sign of a limousine or a black GMC.

"Fucking asshole!" she screams.

Several passing customers stare at her. Raquel ignores them, and hops into her car, making her way back to the beach house. What makes her mad the most is the fact that he has her file with all the necessary paperwork to pave the way for her and her family without any grief. She needs this paperwork.

Raquel races down the PCH. Before she gets to Paradise Cove, she sees the limousine parked on the side of the road with a black GMC escort vehicle nearby.

"What a dick!" she says, and pulls up behind them, waiting to see if he gets out. Both vehicles pull back onto the PCH, and she understands that she should follow them.

So much for my request for the meeting to be at a public place! she thinks.

The limousine and black GMC pull off the road, driving down on Paradise Cove Road. It isn't long before both vehicles come to a stop. Raquel hesitates, at first. She soon throws caution to the wind, and pulls up behind them. She waits for further instructions.

An agent gets out and opens the back door of the limousine. Raquel knows that it's an invitation for her to join the mystery man. She gets out and walks over to the vehicle, promptly getting in. Once inside, she sits quietly while the mystery man contemplates what he wants to say. He hands her a large file, which she gladly accepts.

"We have a deal," he says. "You kept your end of the bargain, so we'll keep ours. You have everything you need in there, including the probation papers. You are free to go."

Raquel looks down at the file and wants to cry. She badly wants to check it out, but she is confident that they will keep their word. It's the way of the Family. She had a speech all prepared, but now she thinks she will just take the file and leave. He reaches over and grabs her arm as she tries to get out.

"No, thank you?" he asks.

Raquel pulls her arm away and turns to face him. "Fuck you, you pathetic piece of shit!"

At that moment, the vehicle's door opens. An agent puts a bullet in his head and one in his chest.

Raquel pulls back against her door, thinking that she is next, but the door closes once more. Moments later, the door behind her opens. A hand reaches out and takes her arm, lifting her to safety.

Totally shaken, Raquel looks up at the agent. She discovers her guardian angel, the assassin. He takes off his dark glasses and smiles.

"You are free to go," he says.

Raquel stands there, frozen in shock. She then moves slowly toward her car, forgetting about the file. The assassin reaches into the limousine and retrieves it before calling out to her.

"You will need this, Raquel," he says, holding out the file.

She hurries back to retrieve it, holding it tight to her chest as she walks back to her car. Turning one last time as she'd done at his house, she looks in his direction. This time, he is still standing there, watching her. He smiles and puts his glasses back on.

"The name is DH. Be good," he says.

"Uncle Carlos?" she asks.

He shakes his head no. "No, he's not the client," he replies.

The limousine and black GMC move away. The mystery man has been sacrificed, though a new mystery begins.

Who is the client? she wonders.

In the end, it really doesn't matter. She is free. She watches as the limousine and black GMC pass her by once more, driving onto the PCH before disappearing altogether.

Raquel looks at the file lying on the passenger seat and screams, "I'm fucking free!"

20

NO TIME LIKE THE PRESENT, Raquel leaves early for the valley. "I'm fucking free!" she shouts.

She makes the long drive through Topanga Canyon, keeping an eye on her speed. She doesn't want to tempt fate and turn this all around.

Raquel arrives at her destination and goes inside. It's not long before there is a knock at the door. She can't get there soon enough. Swinging the door open, she finds her children standing there smiling. These are her children, and the crying begins. The hubby, or soon-to-be ex-hubby, looks solemn and is slightly drunk.

"See you tomorrow," he says as he turns away.

"Hey, you said the weekend!" she shouts, but he continues to the car where his girlfriend sits in a storm of her own.

"It's good, Mom. We're together now," her son says.

Raquel smiles and lets the thunder subside inside her. The night couldn't have gotten any better. They laugh and cry, talking about the future. The kids are all for it. She asks them not to share any plans yet until she has everything all worked out. They agree.

"How long, Mom?" they ask in unison.

"No more than a month, I hope. We can hang out on weekends until then," she assures them.

As it turns out, her ex didn't return as promised. The kids spend the entire weekend with Raquel. She'll have them every weekend for almost five weeks. By then, she's found her leverage and timing. While she's out with the kids one weekend, the bitter girlfriend tries to run her off the road.

Enough is enough. Raquel calls her ex and delivers an ultimatum. The kids are staying with her for good. She will get primary custody and he will sign the papers. To her surprise, he agrees immediately, and her heart hammers with excitement. Raquel takes him back to court and the dumb shit signs away. The deal is sealed.

Raquel has one more thing to do. She needs to go back to Blythe and tell Eric that all is good. When that will be, she can't quite predict, but she knows it has to be done soon.

"I have been justifiably wounded, but motherfucker, I'm alive and kicking!"

Also By Mark Roemmich

"Every day, think as you wake up, today I am fortunate to be alive, I have a precious human life, and I am not going to waste it. I am going to use all my energies to develop myself, to expand my heart out to others; to achieve enlightenment for the benefit of all beings. I am going to have kind thoughts towards others, I am not going to get angry or think badly about others. I am going to benefit others as much as I can." — Dalai Lama

SHINDIG ON THE GREEN is famous for its seasonal festivals and musical venues. Live music and arts are a significant element in this tourism-based economy and surrounding areas. A large crowd of tourists and locals are milling about along the river, experiencing the arts and crafts and food displays, as well as the many single artists and Bluegrass bands featured in the farmer's market atmosphere.

Jacob Labrecque has been coming to the Shindig on the Green since he was a young lad. He is walking with his family, which is made up of a daughter named Amy Harris and her husband, Ray. He was also blessed with a granddaughter named Emily, who is about eight years of age. She is quite small for her age, and she is always sporting a very old-fashioned hat that covers most of her head. It has small flowers on one side, and she will not leave the house without it.

Emily is full of life and leaves her mark everywhere she goes. There is not a person in Asheville that hasn't been touched by Emily Harris in some way. A special aura surrounds her tiny body that radiates outward. She has been diagnosed with a peculiar strain of Leukemia. People like to label her as a Leukemia victim, but she enjoys every present moment of life and doesn't like to be called a victim.

Emily lives the Dalai Lama's philosophy at the young

age of eight. Most people search their whole lives for the wisdom she possesses. Emily struggles with Leukemia, but she transcends her pain by living each day as it comes. When the pain is too great, she goes to her safe place within her hour glass world. She shares this hour glass world with a chosen few, but she always shares her wisdom and love of life. Perhaps when you read her story or see her vision, you too will be affected by Emily Harris. Her story is filled with true emotion reflected in her poems. She will meet a young man that will translate these words—these lyrics—into a song that will become her legacy.

A tempest will be unleashed upon the House of Barrett and the incumbent of the powerful seat of the chairman will lash out at all political foes who challenge . . .

I have been in the rainforest almost three months now, and these little people have accepted me without judgment. They are a simple people trying to survive in a new world. Their home, the rainforest, is being pillaged and raped by progress. They are dying out slowly, but they keep going strong.

I have grown close to them as much as possible. It is difficult, at times, but if I stay the course, I believe that I can come to know them.

They are simple, but their customs and beliefs are complex. I try to understand, but our differences clash greatly. They do as I ask because I ask it, and therefore, they do it. They call me Patron. It's a title of honor, I guess.

When I first arrived I was reticent to stay with them since they are predominantly hunters and practice cannibalism. I have since learned that this inclination has a strange, but propitious, intendment, so I have dismissed it from my thoughts.

A MESSAGE FROM RAQUEL SYRAH

"Who is Raquel?"
That will be the question on everyone's
mind by the end of this first novel.
But truth be told, I am still trying to figure it out,
myself, who I am.

In life, I didn't have it easy, but I have used what I was handed and have overcome adversity in literally all areas. The choice to share my life with the world did not come easy. As a strong independent woman, I carry my own insecurities, fears, worries, and hesitations. I knew that mentally diving into my past would be grueling and painful.

Finding the right person that I could entrust with my deepest, darkest secrets and transpose them on paper would be laborious. After meeting with Mark and his wife, I knew that this fit was meant to be. I knew I'd met the one person who would be able to translate my stories (some dreams and some nightmares) into something infamous and breathtaking.

My hope of opening up and sharing my life events with the world is that somewhere someone can relate to my stories and learn to be brave. That no one should ever feel ashamed of the situations and/or circumstances that have transpired in their lives. As a woman, I've made personal choices that may not be 'socially' acceptable by others, but they did not make me a 'bad' person.

My experiences made me human. And as they say, to err is human, but to forgive is divine. Well, I'm starting my forgiveness with myself.

In life, we all have two choices . . . you can choose to be a victim, or you can choose to be a survivor. Not only have I chosen to be a survivor, I am choosing to be a witness, a teacher, and a mentor to women (and men) of all ages, races, nationalities, and creeds.

I'm here to let the world know that no matter how many lemons are thrown at you in life, everything is easier with a lemon drop martini!

ABOUT RAQUEL SYRAH

Raquel Syrah was raised in the San Fernando Valley. She is, in fact, a real life person, who has overcome adversity and life's obstacles, and has been through many trials and tribulations. She prides herself on the relationship she has with her children and her career.

Working hard, day in and day out, she has always felt that the life she was handed was all for a reason. She's chosen to tell her stories and share her experiences and hope with others. She hopes that others can relate to what she's gone through, and that they, too, can become survivors.

In her free time, she enjoys reading, wine tasting, traveling, and making memories with her children.

Connect with **Raquel Syrah** online via the following social media outlets to keep up-to-date on what's coming next for his books and films.

Email: raquelsyrah@gmail.com
Facebook: https://www.facebook.com/raquel.syrah
Website: http://www.whoisraquel.com
Twitter: https://twitter.com/RaquelSyrah

Connect with **Mark Roemmich** online via the following social media outlets to keep up-to-date on what's coming next for his books and films.

Email: mroemmich@aol.com
Facebook: https://www.facebook.com/authormarkroemmich
Website: http://nhepictures.com
Twitter: https://twitter.com/mroemmich
Goodreads: https://www.goodreads.com/author/show/9023031.Mark_Roemmich

ABOUT THE AUTHOR

Mark Roemmich, President and CEO of Noble House
Entertainment Pictures, has been involved in the pre-
production, production and postproduction of feature films,
television, commercials, PSA docudramas and Visual Effects
since 1969. As the global film industry continues to expand
and mature and new formats are developed, NHEP has
moved quickly to satisfy demand for quality projects.

Roemmich established NHEP in 1985 to develop and
produce feature films, constantly working with prominent
industry professionals to attract projects that are attractive to
both the Major studios and the Mini-Majors. His vision is to
keep NHE flexible and to establish co-production
relationships throughout the world.

Since NHEP's inception, he has written or acquired several
main stream projects for development and production.
Recently, NHEP has entered into co-production relationships
with India/South Africa and Germany to produce and direct
major epics.